Skylar
From one maniac
to another

~ Joe Prosit

MACHINES MONSTERS AND MANIACS

A SHORT STORY COLLECTION

JOE PROSIT

SCI-FI   HORROR   PSYCHO FICTION

CONTENTS

3

Welcome to Mister Smiley's Happy World Theme Park and Fun Land

If robots were humans, this would be a war crime. Murder. Atrocity. Genocide. Something worthy of Nobel Prize winning photography, international peacekeepers, or at least a mass grave. Instead, they got me. Chief called me up, on my day off no less, and sent me out here to the Happy World Theme Park and Fun Land.

I looked down at the bright oval eyes and wide teethy grin of the lone dictator and inhabitant of Happy World, the infamous Mister Smiley. His eyes looked blank, lidless and unblinkable. The smile never faded; it was embossed in the steel head for all time and never needed to rest or take a breath of oxygen. Its steel skin was painted the color of sunshine. The big round head was two times too big for its body and crowned with a cute quaff of hair swooping to the right. It sat in a puddle of rust-orange water, looking up at me with that big stupid smirk. Mister Smiley was dead, but oh so happy to be here anyway.

He wasn't alone. Dozens of identical metal corpses were scattered through the park. Dead Mister Smileys, as far as the eye could see.

"Real cool, dad," Sophie said behind me.

My daughter. Thirteen going on twenty three. She strolled through the concrete path littered with dozens of Mister Smiley robots. Her eyes hid behind dark hair. Her hands burrowed into her pockets. The laces of her shoes dragged through the water, flopped with each step, and frayed a little more each time they were stepped on.

"I thought I told you to stay in the car," I called back. She was supposed to be in school. Was supposed to be home sick in bed. Was supposed to at least be in my police cruiser where I told her to stay put since I got the call to come out and investigate this mess.

"You know, you did promise you'd bring me to Happy World, back when I was five and into this kind of shit," she said.

"Language!" But she had a point. I did make a promise, what felt like a century ago when she was less moody pre-teen and more bouncing pig-tailed ball of pre-school energy. Well, here she was, walking through a field of her old dead heroes. The idea that all this might have actually upset her took way too long to sink in. "Ah shit, honey. I'm sorry."

"Really, dad?" she said as she stepped over one of the lifeless robot mascots. "I don't know if you've noticed, but it's been a while since I watched the Mister Smiley Show."

"Yeah. I've noticed," I said. If she wanted to play the too-cool-for-school act, fine. That worked for me.

I turned and walked deeper into the park and came to what had brought us here. The free fall drop tower, the pinnacle of Happy World, complete with Mister Smiley's face and bright multi-colored pendants. It had toppled like a redwood under a lumberjack's axe, but it was no lumberjack that felled this smiling phallus. Just disrepair, the salty ocean air, and massive structural failure. Dead Mister Smiley robots were scattered along the length of the tower, and at least one other ride had been crushed by the fall. Its base was at the center of the park, and its felled corpse stretched from the center to here, just inside the front gates of Happy World.

"The bigger they are…" I mumbled to myself.

When they cancelled the Mister Smiley Show, the whole Smiley Empire went south quick, fast, and in a hurry. The show went off the air. Then the toys in all the stores hit the discount shelf. Then Mister Smiley's Happy World and Fun Land closed its gates. The stock went tits up and the investors dropped Mister Smiley like a bad habit. But the money had already been spent on the latest endeavor in hi-tech kid's entertainment. Mister Smiley himself was already rolling off the assembly line. Hundreds of robotic mascots, due to hit malls and playgrounds and five year old birthday parties were suddenly as homeless as heroin junkies. So they sent them here to wander through the park for the rest of their days, slowly rusting apart and shorting out and tirelessly encouraging each other to smile and "Make today a happy day!" until they went the way of the drop tower and collapsed.

Somewhere millions of freshman college philosophy students were hammering out think-pieces with Mister Smiley as the ironic main star. For everyone else, he died a long time ago. Life, stardom, and the hearts of millions of TV watching kids across the globe are fickle things.

"Why are they all broken?" Sophie spoke up again as she followed me weaving through the bodies. "I thought robots were supposed to last forever."

"Nothing lasts forever, kiddo," I said. "Cheap production quality, no scheduled maintenance, left out in the rain… Crash a drop tower into the middle of their concentration camp and I figure that took out any that managed to make it this long."

"What about that one?"

I turned back to the entrance of the park, where we'd come in. There was a gate in the ten-foot tall fence that surrounded the park, and the turnstiles and ticket stands inside of that. I had to take a bolt cutter to the chain locking the front gate, and now it hung open just enough for me and Sophie to slip inside. Of course the fence was made up of circular images of Smiley's smiling head, but that's not the one Sophie was talking about.

A lone Mister Smiley robot limped across the wet concrete, dragging one metal foot and hopping with the other as it cut across our path leading back through the gate to my cruiser. It stopped in the middle of the turnstiles and rotated its giant head towards us. It looked at us, all eyes, bulbous nose, and crescent moon mouth. Then it spoke, its voice a distorted and crackling version of the high-pitched siren song of so many Saturday mornings long forgotten. "Hi, everybody. Welcome to Happy World. I want to make you smile!"

"What a fucking disaster," I mumbled and went about fishing a cigarette from a pack.

"Language, dad," Sophie said. "'Sides, he's kinda cute in a lost wet puppy dog sort of way. Can we keep him?"

"Har har," I said and lit my smoke. I looked up to the gray sky as I inhaled. Solid gray cloud cover, the only variation in it were the clouds darker and heavier with rain than the rest. "Never mind that thing. I'd like to get out of here before we get rained on. All I need to do is check out this wrecked tower and confirm there's no human injuries. I can file the report from home."

"What's he doing?" Sophie asked.

"I said never mind that thing." But I did mind it. The surviving Mister Smiley was headed to the front gate of the park, but got caught by one of the turnstiles trying to go out through the entrance. When it pushed and the turnstile refused to rotate, the thing sort of bounced off and tried again. On attempt number three, things got violent. The robot's arms didn't have elbows and its fingers were molded into an immobile ungripping four fingered white glove, so when it started smashing the turnstile to pieces it did so with a series of surprisingly fast and heavy karate chops. Before the turnstile was smashed to pieces, Sophie had let out a yelp and I was at her side, my hand on the butt of my holstered gun.

"Dad?" she said, still thirteen and not yet twenty three.

"Malfunctioned," I said. "We'll stay clear and it won't give us..."

I wanted to finish my sentence and reassure my daughter with the simple notion that if we left Mister Smiley alone, he'd leave us alone. Thing was, Mister Smiley had moved through the turnstile gate to the ten-foot tall fence and was bending the metal bars together like they were bits of shoelace.

"Hey! What's the big idea?" I called to the robot. Did it hear? Could it comprehend human speech? Did it care what I had to say even if it could?

Smiley finished tying the metal bars into a pretzel, effectively sealing us inside the park, and only then turned to address us. "You can never leave," it said in that overdriven guitar voice of his. "I want to make you smile!"

Then he started limping back towards us, both of those white glove hands outstretched towards us.

"Oh-ho-ho," I laughed, gently moved Sophie aside, and drew my .45. "You have no idea how long I've been waiting for this."

"Dad, no," Sophie said, but was too late.

How many episodes of that god-awful show had I endured? How many recitations of stupid catch-phrases and saccharin-sweet songs had bored their way into my skull? How many times did I have to look into those vapid eyes and tolerate that psycho rectus smile? How much money did I spend on toys, posters, pajamas, and books? However much and how many, Mister Smiley was due for some payback.

Three shots. That was it. Each one a blast of thunder in the quiet damp morning. Each hollow point punched through the Mister Smiley's metal face. I had no idea what was inside that spherical head, where its central processor was, or where I should aim to actually kill the robot, but the three holes between those big oval eyes seemed to do the trick. It took one more hop forward, then lost balance and toppled back.

"-the fuck, dad?" Sophie yelled. "What the hell did you do that for?"

I took a nice long drag off my cigarette and flicked ashes from the butt. "Language. Besides, you heard it. He threatened us."

"With what? Making us happy? God forbid," she said, walking away from me, deeper into the park along the felled drop tower. "Jesus, I'm going to be deaf for the rest of my life now."

"Oh, I'm sorry. A minute ago you were telling me how you weren't into this shit anymore. How you were too cool and grown up to like Mister Smiley. Now you're upset I didn't let him bash your brains in?"

"Doesn't mean I wanted to watch you murder him," she mumbled the way teenagers mumble when they want to sneak in the last word. "Can we please just get this over with so we can go home?"

"Yeah, fine," I resigned. "And if it makes any difference, I'll promise not to kill any more of them."

"Just like you promised to bring me here when I was little?" she said.

Now we were bringing up old shit. Fantastic.

I let her have the last punch and followed her as she scuffled along the side of the tower's skeleton towards the center of the park. She had a point. She should be home sick, not wandering through this damp tetanus-infested concentration camp for the robotically and chronically insane. But when the boss called and told me I was the only available detective around, and either I go or it's my badge, well, there we were in what used to be the happiest place on Earth, checking for casualties in the only place in the whole city not occupied by anything close to resembling a human being.

But I'll admit it. I came half out of morbid curiosity. This place was a local legend amongst oddities ever since it closed down and they quarantined their robots inside. For a while, we'd catch neighborhood kids sneaking up to the fences to taunt and throw things at the robots when they were still on their feet. More recently, if you drove by you could occasionally see a lone straggler, lost and confused by its vacant surroundings and insufficient programmings. Now, they all seemed more piles of rust than wandering balls of existential crises.

We passed by a Tilt-a-Whirl that had been repainted in the style of Smiley and Happy World. Lots of white teeth and eyes. Sunshine-yellow faces on the domes of the cars. The ride had been half-crushed when the drop tower came down. Under the wreckage, bare wires and severed hydraulic lines leaked out electrons and vicious red petroleum syrup. A speaker mounted to an upright missed by the tower sparked to life and played the Mister Smiley theme song. The tempo played faster and higher pitched than intended, and then slowed to a crawl like a demon singing a Led Zeppelin song backwards.

"In Happy World Mister Smiley is here for you. He'll make you smile annnnnnnd laaaaaauuuugh annnnnnnnnd plaaaaaaaaaaay aaaaaallllllllllllllllllllll daaaaaaa—"

Another shower of sparks ended the tune. Thank god. The hyper-joyed show tune was bad enough coming through the TV during a Saturday morning hangover. Here? In this museum of lost innocence? It stabbed me like an audible spinal tap.

I didn't realize it until it was gone, but the song was hiding other ambient noises. Noises of crippled metal feet scraping against wet concrete. Plodding flat footsteps followed us along the path. Ungreased metal shoulder joints swung four-fingered gloves. I pivoted and saw four more Mister Smileys on their feet, trailing behind us. It was habit, me reaching for my .45. Sophie's quick move to put her palm on my forearm seemed just as practiced and rote.

"Dad, you promised," she said.

"They're coming for us, Sophie."

Then, from the direction we'd been walking, I heard more scuffling metal feet. I spun. Three more approached from the opposite direction. Stiff metal arms swung in ungreased screeching unison. Those yellowed-but-once-white hands reached out for us. Their eyes were fixed. Their teeth bared. We were surrounded.

"Come smile with us," one said through a rotted speaker.

"Come play."

"It's Happy Time!"

My hand still on the butt of my gun, I pulled at it, but Sophie's hand pressed down on my forearm, keeping the barrel from clearing the holster.

"No, dad!"

"What then?" I demanded.

The Smileys came nearer, closing their perimeter around us.

"Run!" and she took off in the opposite direction of the crushed Tilt-a-Whirl, slipping between two of the automatons.

I rushed after my daughter and shouldered through one of those little bastards along the way. It pawed at me with its round useless fingers but caught nothing.

Ahead of me, Sophie came to a short chain link fence that corralled in the bumper cars. She vaulted over the fence onto the rubberized floor. I followed, climbing over the fence with a little more effort and ache in my bones. The Smileys collapsed their perimeter and followed after us like water flowing from a punctured bladder.

As Sophie weaved between the bumper cars, all of them painted with that same stupid grinning face, I glanced over my shoulder. The robots were against the short fence, and instead of jumping or climbing over it, they were smashing it apart, those stiff elbowless arms acting like metal clubs. It didn't take long for them to reduce the fence to a wreckage. We were trapped again, now between the flat black wall of the backside of the coral and the Smileys who were making quick work of the fence. As it was pummeled to the ground, the Smiley's breached the barrier and stepped onto the rubber floor.

"We love your smile!" they said, emphasizing the word "your" by pointing at me and my daughter with those white hands, some of which were busted apart from clubbing the fence. Instead of articulated pointing fingers, they aimed dangling live wires and shards of white gloves at us.

I took one more step back and bumped against the wall.

"Shit."

"Dad," Sophie said.

"What?" I said. The lead Smiley kicked into the first bumper car and tilted over sideways. More followed. They didn't trip. "God damn it."

"Dad!"

"What?" They were fanning out. Covering our escape routes to the left or right. "Fuck!"

"Dad!" she said and backhanded my shoulder. I turned and she found a service door leading out of the back of the bumper car coral. She had it cracked open and was already halfway through when we met eyes. "Language," she said and slipped through.

Smart ass. Worse than her old man.

On the other side of the door was some neglected landscaping, dead bushes and soggy wood chips. We stumbled our way through and I slammed the door behind us.

"Good luck with door knobs you albino sausage-fingered bastards," I said.

"There's more," Sophie said.

Past the shrubbery was another concrete path winding through the park. And sure enough, more of the perpetually manic mascots approached from either direction. I took a quick survey of our new surroundings. Smileys to the right and Smileys to the left. In front of us... In front of us was the haunted house, stylized in the Happy World theme, but instead of displaying Mister Smiley it featured his black mirror twin: Mister Spooky. While Smiley's quaff went right, Spooky's went left. Smiley was a ball of sunshine. Spooky was the color of a purple bruise. The crescent moon mouth was identical to Smileys but turned upside down into a sneer. Spooky wore sharp eyebrows aiming hateful eyes downward. I remembered Smiley's warning from those long-ago TV episodes. Only one thing can ruin a smile: fear.

Perfect.

"There," I said. "Into the haunted house."

For once, Sophie didn't argue. We charged across the path and through the rows of metal-barred waiting lines. The ride was one of those with cars not that dissimilar to the Tilt-a-Whirl cars, these ones set on tracks that snaked through the haunted house. Their half-globe backs were painted with Spooky's face instead of Smiley's. We decided to skip the unpowered cars and push through the big wooden double doors leading into the fun house on foot.

It was quiet inside. Dark. The decorations and automatons along the tracks were dead and motionless. The jump scares lacked any jump. We could tell the paint on the walls was blacklight reactive, but only the dim of an overcast sky seeped through the drafts. It was all as unsettling as a painting with eyes that follow you across a room. Things were leering. Waiting. A lot of cartoonish thunder clouds, hordes of yellow eyes on black background, mangy cats caught with their backs arched mid-hiss, and of course Mister Spooky himself. He peeked over wooden fences and out of oversized sewer pipes that dripped green slime. We crept through the maze on careful and quiet feet. All this potential motion paralyzed for God knows how long was somehow creepier than the actual ride could have ever been.

"I think we lost them," I said after we'd turned the second hairpin and heard no sounds of approaching automatons. "Maybe Mister Spooky is keeping them at bay."

"Maybe it was you shooting him in the face," Sophie said, her small voice echoing through the winding canal of the haunted house.

"Could be."

"God, dad. You're such an ass," she said. "You can't solve every problem with violence, you know?"

"Well, when all you got is a hammer, every problem tends to look like a round-headed smiling hellspawn I thought died a half a decade ago," I said. "Listen, let's just get back to the squad car, get you out of here, and I'll call for back-up."

"You always hated him," she mumbled. I didn't hear her the first time, so I asked her what she said and she came back louder. "You always hated him. Even when I was a little kid and loved Mister Smiley you hated him. Wouldn't be around when the show was on. Complained everytime mom would buy me a Smiley toy. Made excuses when I asked to come here to Happy World. You thought I never noticed? Well, congratulations. You raised me from a baby into a bitch."

"Hey! Keep the volume down!"

"Well, what do you want me to be, dad? A brooding angry asshole like you? Or a little girl who still watches Mister Smiley?"

"I— Really? Right now? We have to have this conversation right now?"

I saw Sophie take a deep breath in preparation for her next verbal salvo, but her words got caught in the breech. Instead of opening her mouth, her eyes grew wide and alert. With the break in noise, it didn't take me long to realize why. Those big double doors that led into the haunted house just creaked open, and now metal feet plodded and scraped against the floor.

It still didn't stop Sophie from saying her peace. Her whispered words somehow related more fury than any shouts ever could. "You always hated Mister Smiley."

I drew my .45 and whispered back, "You're god damn right I did."

"Dad!" my daughter exclaimed in whispers. "You promised!"

I leaned close to her, our words furious but quiet. "And what should I do? Smile at them to death? I'm going to get us out of here. That's the only promise I'm going to make and the only promise I'm going to keep. I love you and I'm going to keep you safe. Get it?"

"Dad!" Sophie kept on. The Smileys were getting closer, working their way through the maze. I could hear their squeaking limbs echo down the trail. "God damn it, dad. Listen to me! There's not enough bullets in your gun to shoot them all. You saw how many there are!"

"We'll see about that," I said, fixated down the tunnel, my gun held out at arm's length.

It wasn't until they came around the turn that I realized just how many there were and how right Sophie was. They shuffled around the bend like cattle, so crammed together their heads bonked into each other as they waddled. Each face identical, huge half-circle smiles and desperate eyes, some with orange tears where rain water had left lines of rust trailing down from their eyes. Their insane expression of joy all the more senseless when surrounded by the creepshow decor of Mister Spooky's hell ride.

They stopped in unison, as if led by one mind.

"Come play with us," the Smiley most front and center said. "Smile with us. We want to make you happy forever!"

I re-gripped the gun. Sophie's whispered were laced with terror. "Don't. There's too many. For once, just trust me."

I grimaced and lowered the barrel of a gun just a few inches.

The herd of happy robots lifted up their white gloved hands and restarted their shuffle towards us, ready to inflict their will upon us.

I raised the gun back up, ready to fire at the lead Smiley. Sophie stepped around me and threw her arm over mine, forcing the barrel down and away. Then she spoke with a syrupy sweetness I hadn't heard from her since… How long had she been all teenage-angst? Since long before then. "Hi, Mister Smiley! I'm so happy to be here!"

The Smileys stopped. Obsolete processors spun inside those stupid metal domes. The lead Smiley seemed to come to a conclusion first. It spun its outstretched arms sideways into a perverse cruciform, backhanding the nearest two other Smileys. A split second later, like a flock of starlings devoid of grace and beauty, the other Smileys mimicked the gesture. All those white gloved hands spread from that zombie/Frankenstein pose to arms wide open. At the back of the pack, a Smiley caught a back-hand and toppled over on its ass.

"We love it when you're happy!" the lead Smiley said, quoting its own catch phrase. Like an echo chamber, the other Smileys repeated the phrase a moment later. "Have a grrrrrreat happy day!" They all said, waving at us with their stiff arms and stupid balloon hands.

"You got to be kidding me," I said, just loud enough for Sophie to hear.

"Just smile, dad," she said, her words sounding happy, but laced with fear a millimeter below the surface. She slid her hand down to my .45 and tried slipping it from my grip. I resisted. Of course I'd resist. "Trust me," she said, and smooth like water, I let her take my gun and holstered it in her own hip pocket.

She was right. If I kept it, it wouldn't be long before I broke my smile and the cease-fire all at once.

I forced a grin at the Smileys. I doubted whatever AI resided in the machines was smart enough to discern an insanity-inspired smirk and true contentment. I bared my teeth, leered at them, and that was enough.

The Smileys in the back of the pack turned as if suddenly bored, and waddled back down the tunnel towards the entrance. A few others muddled about. The lead Smiley continued to lock eyes and engage us.

"What makes you happy? Not Mister Spooky! No!" the thing chuckled. It's laugh was an inhuman robotic insult to humor. "I know what makes you happy. Mister Smiley makes you happy!"

"Just keep smiling," Sophie said, "and back away."

We moved deeper into the ride, both of us grinning like a pair of straight-jacket mental patients. It was maniacal, but effective. The Smileys who stayed in the tunnel lost their sense of purpose and just milled about, being aggressively joyous towards us and each other. We painted happiness on our own stupid faces and snuck away.

Along the path to the haunted house exit, we came across more Smileys, and as long as we mimicked their rictus, they let us pass by, inches from them.

When we came to the exit double doors, the dim sunlight that made its way through the overcast clouds strained our eyes. It was bright out here, compared to the dank tomb that was Mister Spooky's haunted house. Still, there was nothing less spooky about our surroundings outside the ride. We hid in the darkness because of what the overcast sunlight had to offer: flocks of purposeless Mister Smileys meandering through their dead comrades. They stayed that way, impotent and aimless, just so long as we kept our grins pulled back to our ears.

We shuffled through the park back towards the entrance, through the ambling robots, warding them off with plastered-on grins like they were vampires and our teeth were crosses. If one didn't notice our grin, it turned towards us to investigate. One drew near, so we turned to it and smiled as big as we could. Then it wandered off, satisfied.

"Are you... happy?" one of them asked. We spun and showed it our teeth, and it responded, "I am so happy that you're happy!" Then it continued on its indiscernible way.

They milled about, dense enough to never give us a break. When I chanced a glance away from them to my daughter, I saw she had tears running out from the corners of her eyes.

"Dad, my cheeks hurt," she managed between clenched teeth.

"Mine too. We're almost there, sweetie. We'll jump the turnstiles and climb over the fence, jump in my cruiser, and leave this place and never come back. For now, just stay happy."

She laughed, but not in a funny way. In a tormented sort of way.

The front gate was just ahead.

We saw the turnstiles, the mangled outer gate, and my car just beyond that. But there was one more robot in front of the exit. The others seemed to have drifted away, preferring the deeper recesses of Happy World than this one. This one was different.

His metal skin was painted purple. Where Mister Smiley's hair quaffed right, this one went left. Thick black eyebrows angled down, connecting with its bulbous nose. It's crescent moon mouth was turned down. Mister Spooky.

"Look at you happy little kids," the robot said, standing defiantly between us and the exit. "I don't like it when kids are happy. I like it when you're afraid. Are you afraid now?"

"Lie to him," I told Sophie. "Just like in your shows."

"I can feel that you're afraid," Mister Spooky said, then chuckled high-pitched and insane like a helium-huffing studio audience. "I like when you're afraid. You can't be happy when you're afraid."

"Happiness chases away the fear, right? Just like when you were a little girl," I said.

Then I saw the fake smile drop from her face. Under it was her unmasked true emotions. Not fear, but pent up rage.

"News flash, dad. I'm not a little girl anymore," Sophie said.

She drew my .45 from her hip pocket and leveled the sights at Mister Spooky. She'd paid attention when I'd brought her to the range. I admit, her stance and posture weren't textbook, but her aim was dead-eye. Mister Spooky took three rounds to his globe head, fell over backwards, and bounced off the dead Mister Smiley I'd knocked out earlier.

They all go down the same.

The three shots echoed like thunderclaps through the amusement park. Like a dinner bell for the starving masses. Dozens of Smileys all turned towards us. They locked on to us like heat-seeking missiles. How they selected a leader was a mystery to me but immediate. One of them stepped forward and spoke for the horde.

"Those kiddos aren't happy. Hey everyone! Can we make them smile?"

I think we figured out why the Smiley Empire crumbled. Why these automatons never saw mass distribution to all those fast food restaurants, strip malls, and birthday parties. They had a unique sense of childhood entertainment. Sophie and I, we had a different sense.

"Run!" she said and took off.

I followed.

She stuck the .45 over her shoulder and fired blindly at the encroaching stumbling herd. She was right though. There wasn't enough bullets in the gun to put them all down. When it went dry she dropped it on the ground and vaulted over the turnstiles. I slipped through them right along side of her. We hit the border fence at a sprint and started scaling up the Mister Smiley designed metal work. The nearest Smiley smashed through the turnstile just as we reached the top of the fence. Those permanently outstretched arms were reaching for us when we went over the top. Their smooth hands grabbed at us through the fence when we landed on the other side, but couldn't flex to rake us in. We backed away from them and knew we were out of their reach, for now.

"Come play with us."

"We want to make you happy."

"Smiles chase away your fears."

"No one can make you afraid while I'm around."

Sophie regarded them once more as we back stepped to the cruiser. "Fuck you, Mister Smiley. I never liked you anyway."

We climbed inside and shut the doors behind us, muffling out their desperate pleas.

"They're going to smash through the fence," I said. "They'll escape into the city."

"Call it in, dad. There's other cops who can take care of them," Sophie told me. "Today's our sick day."

Stilt Walkers

ONE – LITTLE BUDDY LAB RAT

Amber sucked in a quick gasp of air.

"Was I asleep?"

If she had drifted off, it hadn't been for long. A dirty stuffed toy mouse sat in her lap having fallen from her fingers. The toy was a prize won from the arcade crane machine. She picked it up and dusted it off. "You're supposed to keep me awake, Mister Jonesy. Don't let me do that."

Quiet suburban homes sat like uniform tombstones across the neighborhood from her perch. There were just a few floor plans in the whole development, each flipped, mirrored, turned and painted different colors to fake variation. This wasn't her treehouse. The treehouse and split-entry below belonged to an old retired couple with no kids. But nobody used the treehouse besides her, so in a way, it kind of was hers. Her mom's house, where she still lived, was a few blocks over. But this was one of her sentry posts she'd picked out to keep watch. To watch for them.

"See any of them yet, Jonesy?"

The mouse didn't answer. Crickets and frogs sustained their midnight anthem of creeks and croaks.

She peered out from the treehouse and scanned the night. So far, all clear. There was no door or window at the back of the treehouse, and she considered removing a board from the back wall so she could see in all directions. But she was over eighteen now. A legal adult. That meant if she got busted for trespassing or vandalism, she'd get arrested for real. She couldn't afford to get locked up, not in some windowless cell where it'd be too easy to sleep.

"Can't sleep, Mister Jones. If we sleep, we get weak. We can't see them and we sure as shit can't stop them."

The stuffed animal was clearly a mouse. Blue fur. Cute button nose. Round ears. Big smile. A furry tail that clung to the body by just a few threads. It wasn't meant to be a rat, but that's how she thought of it. Mister Jones, her little buddy lab rat.

"They'll come, no matter what. But if we sleep there will be no one to see them, and no one to stop them. They'll plant their bad ideas in our dreams, trick us into thinking they're nightmares instead of mental poison. That's how come people are evil, right Jonesy? All those bad thoughts injected into our brains at night. They're behind it all. They got me once, Jonesy, but never again, huh?"

Jonesy smiled.

The wee hours ticked by, each second building up the abilities inside of her, abilities anyone might have, if only they had the guts. The guts, and the knowledge of what sleeplessness would bring. Late at night, when everyone else was tucked in their beds and she and Jonesy were the only ones still awake, the night would pull back its thin black veil and the stilt walkers would wander out.

"I know you're with me, Mister Jones," she slurred.

Jonesy was a rat, not a mouse, because they didn't do sleep deprivation studies on mice. They used rats. They used rats and they put them in buckets half-full of water with only a little platform in the middle so when the rat tried to fall asleep it would fall off the platform and into the water and have to climb back onto the platform and learn to stay awake, indefinitely. That's who Jonesy was. A partner in her self-imposed insomnia.

So what if she was an adult who talked to stuffed animals and hid out in treehouses all night? She knew what she was doing. Knew it was important. Knew she could save them all.

If she could just stay awake.

"I need my own water bucket, Jonesy," she said and petted the rat. Caffeine got her by for a while. But inevitably came the crash. She needed something more reliable. More long term. She needed discipline.

If she'd been disciplined before maybe things would be different.

She arched her back. Yawned. Twisted her torso around to the left and right, popping a few vertebrae on the second twist. Daybreak was just an hour or so away. They never came out during the day. All the real bad ideas come at night. She looked through the treehouse doorway, then the little window to the right, then to her—

Amber froze. All she could hear were muffled sounds as if heard through wads of cotton and a high-pitched violin note. Her heart thumped like hooves in a stampede. Her fingernails dug into Jonesy.

The stilt walker traipsed down her street, two blocks over. Its torso, the shape of a blood-filled wood tick, seemed to float above the rooftops, weightless on the thin vertical spider legs. Its clusters of glistening eyes were obsidian and almost invisible against its black body, but she saw how it turned and focused on each house it passed. It was perusing, like an old woman shopping for a purse, slow and patient for just the right one. Javelin-sized whiskers protruded from under its mouth like a beard as it sniffed each house until it found the one it liked.

A split-entry with new plastic siding.

And kid's toys in the yard.

"Mister— Mister Jo— Mister Jones…" she searched for air to fill her lungs and the strength to push it out.

The stilt walker pivoted around the split-entry, sniffing and looming near an upstairs window. It extended a black penial tube from under its body. The tube snaked down between its legs and out to feel the plastic siding like a blind man without a cane. The tip of the tube groped around the edges and crevasses until it found a cracked bedroom window. Then it slipped inside to do its business.

TWO – WAKEFULNESS

Oppression. Murder. Rape. War. Genocide. This is where those things came from. From the stilt walkers.

Like electricity applied to a machine, Amber's nerves finally sparked. She scattered to her feet and out of the treehouse. The ladder, just two by fours nailed to the tree trunk, was half-rotted and half-swallowed by the growth of the trunk, but Amber knew which boards to put weight on and which ones to—

Her foot slipped on the dew-wet smooth wood. One hand lost grip of a board. Her other hand let go of Jonesy and flailed. Too late. She was suspended in a single moment that felt like zero gravity. A second ticked by. Then she hit and every square inch of air escaped her lungs. Stars exploded in her eyes. Mister Jonesy bounced off her chest and into the grass.

But she didn't lose consciousness. Didn't black out. Didn't sleep.

Amber staggered up, dizzy, delirious, fighting to get air back into her lungs and panicked with the very real feeling that she might never breathe again. The fear didn't subside so much as it was overwhelmed by her stronger need to accomplish the task at hand. A gate leading out the backyard was just across the lawn. She zombie-walked a few steps in its direction, her air coming back to her in short shallow gasps. Almost to the fence, she turned back.

"Huuuuup," she sucked in air. "Jo— huuuuuuup. Jonesy. Huuuuuup."

She ran back for the rat lying in the grass. As she picked him up, she got her first real breath. The stars faded from her vision.

"Come on, Jonesy. It's not too late."

Her feet shuffled and skipped through the wet grass to the gate. When she busted through, something about the action let her replenish her lungs, her strength, her vitality. Amber broke into a sprint, cutting across a street and through yards. Between houses, she saw the stilt walker again, looming outside of the cracked window. Its fleshy tube moved bulges down its length like a boa constrictor vomiting up a parade of mice.

"Hey!" she yelled at the stilt walker. Then, to anyone who might hear, "Wake up! It's here! It's poisoning you!"

She charged through the last pair of yards onto her street. She rounded the corner of the last house and jumped a curb-side rose bush. Her All Stars smacked against the blacktop and squeaked to a stop, one on either side of the yellow center line.

Amber shot out her palm, fingers splayed wide open, Jonesy held back close to her heart like a shield. Every ounce of wakefulness she'd saved up, every bit of strength left in her, she aimed it out through her palm towards the monster. She stood firm, her eyes crushed shut, teeth bared and clinched together, her lungs straining to pump air in rapid short breaths. Something glowed through her eyelids.

Brighter. Brighter. The wakefulness radiated out of her hand towards the stilt walker, warding it away from the house and the family inside. She was sure of it. Until she heard the screeching brakes of a car coming to run her down. The car lurched to a stop. She pried open an eye just a crack to see what she feared: the glow wasn't coming from her, it was coming from a pair of damn headlights. The stilt-walker, hidden behind the glare of the lights had probably moved on to its next victim by now. She hadn't created the glow, and she hadn't stopped the monster.

"Hey, are you alright?" a man called from the car.

"Slept too much," she mumbled, draining like a battery. "Have to save up more..."

She staggered, clutched Jonesy for support. Gravity went lopsided. Her upheld arm went limp. Her foot reached out for more stable terrain and failed to find it. Amber spilled down to the pavement and out of the shine of the two hi-beams. Jonesy bounced out of her hand. He landed butt down, facing her, the stitched on smile as permanent as his wakefulness.

"Damn it, Jonesy. We almost—" A deep wheeze to pull in air. "—had him."

THREE – TOXIC THOUGHTS

"Are you getting enough sleep?"

Amber roused herself. She was in the college career counselor's office. The man's name was Gene. This had something to do with picking out a major? There was a coffee pot in the corner of the office. Black as tar and out of reach. She needed Jonesy.

"Listen, Amber. You're only in your first semester and your grades are looking... Well, compared to your entrance exam scores—" the counselor was saying. Gene was a clean guy. Starched shirt. A dress-right-dress work space. She couldn't help but notice his cheeks still waxy and wet from a shave, except one spot he'd missed under his chin.

"I slept some," she stifled a yawn. She didn't add that it was only by accident and only during her last lecture. A morning class. Big auditorium. Only the stage was lit.

"Last time we talked you mentioned you were still dealing with what happened at the end of high school."

The accident. But to call it an accident wasn't fair. She'd been instructed and trained and warned. She'd known all about the dangers of distracted driving since she was sixteen. But she made that decision. A decision injected into her through a long black tube that had slipped into her room at night. A bad decision from a bad creature.

Since then, her piece of shit Toyota Corolla stayed parked along the curb in front of her mom's house. The windshield was still cracked and the passenger's headlight was busted out. She'd sell it if only someone would buy it. In the meantime, she left it parked there, unlocked with the keys in the cup holder, waiting for someone to steal it.

"Have you considered seeing a counselor?"

Amber's fingers worried away at the zipper pull on her sweatshirt. She wanted it to be Jonesy. "Aren't you a counselor?"

"I mean a mental health professional," the counselor said. "Some of the things we've discussed are well beyond my skill set. I'm here to help you prepare yourself for your—"

"They're not hallucinations," Amber cut him off.

"I didn't say—"

"The stilt walkers. I'm not dreaming them up. I *wish* I was, but you can see as well as I can just how bad things are. People are sick, poisoned, their thoughts are toxic, filled to the brink with hate. One of them got to me and look what happened. One of them will get to you too."

"This is exactly what I'm talking about," Gene sighed, more to himself than to her.

"How am I supposed to sleep while I know they're out there? How am I supposed to ignore what I see, when I know what they can do, when I've seen the results of their work first hand?" Amber heard her words slur, so this time she made sure to speak clearly. "I have this ability, and I have a responsibility to use it. It's all I can do after what I let them make me do. I owe it."

"Amber, I am really not qualified to address these sorts of feelings," the counselor said, resigned.

"You could fight them too, if you had the balls," she said. "But you'd rather sleep and let the evil of the world infect us all."

The counselor rocked forward in his chair and leaned against the desk. The old wood creaked under his weight. Amber locked eyes with him. He looked appalled by her, but also concerned. What did she look like? She knew her skin was dry and pale. Her eyelids hung loose, red like a basset hound's. Her mouth was agape. White crude crusted to the corners of her mouth. Zombie queen meets heroin addict.

"How long has it been?" he asked.

"Saw one last night."

"No. How long since you last slept? Really slept, like the whole night through?"

Not long enough. She still wasn't spotting them until almost morning, when the rising sun was ready to chase them off. If she could store up more of her wakefulness during the day she could draw them out sooner. Her thoughts wandered to the water bucket they used on the lab rats. She needed something like that. Something that wouldn't let her nod off.

"Amber?"

"Huh?" Right. The counselor, staring her in the face.

"This will kill you," Gene said.

"People have already died. But nobody else has to. Not anymore."

Amber had done her research, had read and re-read all the studies. The lab rats in the buckets suffered damage to the cortical memory networks. Loss in spatial learning and synaptic plasticity. Depression and hallucinations. Elevated blood pressure. Weight gain. Eventually death. But no humans. No human on record ever died from sleep deprivation. She wasn't going to die. And Jonesy, since he really was just clothe and stuffing, wasn't going to die. And if she did her job right, nobody else would die either.

"You need to go to the Student Services office and ask them about seeing a mental health provider. There are resources available to you. Some at low or no—"

"I should get back to class," Amber stood up and picked a Styrofoam cup off the stack next to the coffee machine.

"Amber—"

The coffee was black. Burnt. Gritty with grounds. She poured the sludge into the cup. No cream. No sugar.

"You don't need—"

The first sip burnt her tongue and mouth.

"Amber, you need sleep."

The sludge went down her throat.

"Jesus Christ," he mumbled and looked away.

"Thanks, doc," Amber said. "Our little talks, they always help."

"I am not in any way, shape, or form a doctor," he was saying when she left the office.

FOUR – ABSOLUTION

Another class. Another monotone voice. Another dimly lit auditorium.

She fought to stay awake. The veil between consciousness and dreams wore silk-thin. In her dreams, Amber saw them against the backdrop of storm clouds rolling in at night. A dozen stilt walkers stalked through the houses, cul de sacs, over a middle school.

Lightning flashed and she was inside the school, in a classroom filled with desks and kids. Outside it rained on the playground. Inside, the kids were playing a game. Heads up Seven up. The kids sitting at their desks had their heads down buried in their arms and they stuck out a fist with a raised thumb. Other kids snuck through the rows and gently pressed down random thumbs. The boys picked their friends. The girls picked the boys they liked. Amber peeked up from her elbow. A stilt walker hung over them from the impossibly high classroom ceiling and watched the game approvingly.

The stilt walker glared down upon them, its beady eyes reflecting flashes of lightning coming through the window. Come on, children. Time to guess. Who snuck by your house late at night while you were sleeping and pressed your thumb down? You only get one guess. Who was it? Tina? Stacey? Maybe Tommy? It couldn't have been the twenty foot demon creature with the long black tendril creeping through your window. Guess!

Her head tipped over sideways and Amber snapped awake.

Back at the community college. Back in the dim auditorium. The teacher still prattling on about US History. Or was it Art Appreciation? No, this was Intro to Psych. Wasn't it? She checked her notes.

Not too many words there. Mostly doodles on the ragged spiral bound notebook. A drawing in the center of the page. A cross section of the bucket with the pedestal in the middle just big enough for a rat to sit on its hind legs. And below the pedestal? In the sleep studies they used water to keep the rat awake, but in her drawing it was different. In her drawing, surrounding the little rodent on its little pedestal were rows and rows of sharp pointy spikes.

"That's it Mister Jonesy," she whispered. Jonesy was deep inside her backpack under her seat. That didn't matter though. She knew he heard her. "I think that's the trick."

\#

"Amber," Gene the career counselor said, leaning against the front of his desk again. "I'd like to introduce you to someone. This is Laura, and she's a mental health counselor from Lutheran Social Services. They offer free consultations for people in your financial situation."

"Hi, Amber."

Laura from Lutheran Social Services sat in a chair parked at the side of the desk. The thin woman's eyes were concerned, sympathetic, imploring, impossibly white as if she bleached them each night before bed.

"I'm not Lutheran," Amber said. This was an ambush. The career counselor had tricked her. Caught her off guard after class and dragged her back into his office. And for what? To have this woman ask her if she'd found Jesus?

Laura smiled politely. "I'm a part of the social outreach program. Doesn't matter what church you belong to or what you believe. I'm here to help."

"Help how? If it's really that big of a deal, I can pick out a major."

Laura drew in and let out a long breath. "Amber, I'm not the type to beat around the bush. I'm not going to ask you about your mother or any of those sorts of questions. When I see trauma in a client's past, I believe it's best to address it directly."

"Okay," Amber's lips fumbled out the words. Her face was numb when she talked and hung slack whenever she didn't. She knew how she looked. It was painted in Laura's wet sympathetic eyes.

"This past May you were involved in an accident," Laura from Lutheran Social Services said. "There was a fatality. A man on a bicycle rode across an intersection when you had a green light."

"It was my fault," Amber said. "If you're going to try to tell me it wasn't, I've heard it all before. But you weren't there."

"The police report says you had a green light. The bicyclist had a 'Don't

Walk' signal he ignored," Laura calmly explained.

"I was looking at my phone," Amber said. The words were becoming harder to get out. Her throat was dry like sandpaper. It was the sleep deprivation. Nothing more. "I— " Throat too dry. Too tight. She tried again. "I never did that before. I knew I wasn't supposed to. But… some *thing* put the idea in my head. That I could ge by with it."

"So you blame yourself for the accident," Laura said.

"No."

"But you just said—"

"It wasn't my idea to do that. I was always a careful driver. I never did that before. Something told me to do that."

Laura lifted her penciled-on eyebrows. Gene gestured and mimed to the woman as if to say, "Here it is. Here's the thing I told you about."

"Still, you feel like you need to make amends," Laura said. "You want absolution."

"I told you I'm not fucking religious."

"But you seek forgiveness, don't you? You wish you could take the memories away, or do something to rectify the injustice."

"I can fix it."

"Fix a fatality? Death is permanent."

These people. They prod her like a mob armed with spears. All day, from all sides. If she really wanted to know, fine, Amber would tell her.

"They come out every night, whether or not I can see them and whether or not you believe it. They stride through the night, picking this house, not picking this one, stopping at this one tonight and then skipping four blocks over the next night. Random. Lethal. You'll never see them. Never hear them. When you're sleeping alone in your bed thinking you're having a nightmare, they will come. And don't worry, doc. If they haven't visited you yet, if there's parts of your soul they haven't charred black, don't worry. They'll come. They'll move through your neighborhood like silent insect sentinels, and one of them will stop outside your window, and it will slip its leathery dick into your bedroom and into your skull, and it will impregnate you with the most vial, filthy, nasty things you've ever thought. And when you wake up it will be gone, and you'll disregard it cause you'll be sure it was just a bad dream. But the thoughts it left will still be inside of you, like eggs laid in your ear canal. Until one day they hatch, and you act them out. And maybe it will be something small and lazy. Something other people will tell you not to blame yourself for, but it will end in shame and regret and misery and death. I fucking promise you."

"You're staying up at night?" Laura asked, her face stoic and marble-like. "To watch for these creatures?"

Amber laughed. She didn't know why. "You want me out there, doc. You need me out there. For you. For your family. Do you have kids, doc?"

"Untreated sleep deprivation can be lethal. Did you know that, Amber?" Laura asked.

"Not to humans. Just to lab rats. They've done studies."

"It's true," Laura said. "No human has ever died in a laboratory sleep study. But there's certain things scientists can do to rats that ethics won't allow them to do to humans."

"Cowards." They'd rather get their beauty sleep and stay weak than face the stilt walkers.

Laura's bleach-white eyes pleaded. "Amber, if you keep this up, it will kill you."

"You're all cowards."

FIVE – WHERE DAYLIGHT MEETS DREAMS

Amber didn't sleep. The wakesfulness was building up inside of her. She could feel it like a glass of water filled to the brink.

In her house just as dusk was painting the sky red, she laid out a white button-up shirt on the bathroom counter. Mister Jonesy sat on the counter too, watching her work. She picked up a long needle from her mother's sewing kit. She tried to be careful, but her hands trembled as she weaved the needle in and out of the stiff collar. Then she threaded another. And another. When she added the last one, the whole collar was lined with the longest and sharpest of the needles, all pointed up around the neck like the prongs of a king's crown. She picked up the shirt and whipped it around her body like a cape. Her arms slipped in the sleeves. Her fingers, numb with fatigue, managed each button all the way up to the top and fastened the collar tight around her neck. The needles rested flat against her skin.

She bent her neck in each direction until she felt the sharp poke of the pins. When she bent forward, one of the longer ones got her good and drew blood.

"Ow," she whispered. She pressed against the tiny hole to staunch the bleeding. Mister Jonesy looked up at her with his solid unblinking eyes. "One more thing, Jonesy. Just to make sure it works."

Amber turned off the bathroom light and the room fell into absolute darkness. There, alone, unobserved and consumed in darkness she had a deep and sudden temptation to lay down and sleep. It would be easy. She'd have to take the shirt with the needles off first, but that wouldn't take more than a few seconds. Then she could sleep, and sleep for a long time. Maybe, after enough rest, all these problems would disappear and she could remember what it was like to be normal again. Did she choose to close her eyes, or was it just fatigue? They closed, and there was no difference. Everything was dark. Still, those dreams were waiting for her just on the other side of the veil of consciousness.

The steering wheel of her car. The dashboard. A text alert from friends since forgotten on her cell phone. A flash of movement above the dash. A guy on a bike. Broken glass and blood.

Amber opened her eyes in the pitch-black bathroom. No difference. Only now she knew she couldn't sleep. Not yet. Couldn't play in her dreams just yet.

She exhaled. "Gotta give it a try, Mister Jonesy. Can't let much out, but I have to know it's in there," she said and closed her eyes again. No temptation of sleep this time. She lifted her palms up in front of her face, her neck straight and rigid to avoid the needles. She crammed her eyes shut and concentrated as hard as she could.

The bathroom began to glow a dull red, then a brighter orange like the coils of an electric space heater. The shapeless glow took form behind her closed eyelids. Two palms. Ten fingers spread wide open. Like an image seen through a thermal sensor.

"That's enough," Amber said, cutting it off, and flicking on the light. It was instantly bright again, and she had to squint her eyes to see. The stuffed toy mouse—the rat, still sat on the counter. "Got to save it up, Jonesy. For when we need it later."

#

The needles did their work. Whenever she drooped they stabbed her awake deep into the night.

Amber watched from her rooftop. Over the course of hours, traffic dwindled from steady to sporadic to vaccuumous. The moon crawled up the sky. Mister Jonesy, held close to her, never blinked and never slept. He'd been classically conditioned in his bucket not to fall asleep a long time ago. For Amber, her conditioning was just beginning. Her eyelids felt heavy like cinder blocks, and if she could have laced sewing needles through them to keep them apart, she would have.

Instead, she sat on the slope of her roof with the spikes surrounding her collar prodding her each time she moved. Every time she turned her neck, each time she craned up or down, they rubbed the skin a little redder and a little rawer.

Hours passed without a single sighting, and her invention got its first real test. Reality gave way to delirium and Amber's head fell forward, hard. Two sewing needles stabbed deep into her skin. The sensation was so instantaneously painful she jerked her head back and got pokes from the needles in the back of her collar almost as deep as the ones in front. That brought her back to full consciousness, as alert as a rabbit in a field full of foxes. She brought her hand up to the skin next to her Adam's apple. Her fingers came away red and wet.

"Jesus, Jonesy," she said. "Remind me not to do that again."

Mister Jonesy didn't reply. His eyes were sewn open. For him, this was old hat.

Amber sighed and shuffled her butt, trying to get a little more comfortable on the shingles. Where were they? She knew they were out there, already stalking through the housing and picking their victims like quiet kids pressing down thumbs in a classroom; she just couldn't see them yet. Each hour meant another house infected with their evil. She couldn't wait much longer. She had to draw them to her. They always came closest to the dawn, when she was the most tired, when she balanced exactly right along the razor's edge between awake and sleep. It was only when she was her most vulnerable that she could see them, intercept them and intervene. Right at that place where daylight met dreams.

She had to give them something. Had to present to them an easy target. A fragile mind for them to infect. Amber never learned to meditate. Never did yoga or any of that other stuff that might have taught her how to control her mind and set it in the place for a trap. So instead, she talked herself through the Hollywood pseudo-spiritual Jedi/Kung Fu version of meditation.

"Center yourself. Clear your mind. Think of nothing. Breathe. Let the bastards come to you," she whispered. She wouldn't allow herself to close her eyes. Just blink after heavy blink. She breathed. Focused. Not so much as to bring out her stored wakefulness, but enough to call out to them with her mind. Weak thoughts. Selfish thoughts. Thoughts that wanted sleep above all else. "Come my way and infect me with your evil. I'm ready for it, you sons of bitches."

Around her, the crickets and frogs silenced their nighttime anthem. The buzz of a transformer went mute. Cool wind brushed past her ears. Something slow and plodding moved behind her. Amber sensed it more than heard it, but she knew exactly what it was

.

SIX – "THIS WILL KILL YOU"

She fixed her eyes straight ahead. Across the housing development, others emerged from the inky darkness of night. Thick bulbous bodies on impossibly thin and sharp legs. A radio tower blinked its warning light and reflected red off their glistening backs. They moved over rooftops like black Nazi zeppelins in the distance. Steady. Silent. Probing each residence for mental and moral weaknesses.

But those stilt walkers didn't concern her nearly as much as the one creeping up behind her back. The sensation of a dozen whiskers as thick as hemp ropes stretching out to her. They smelled her, tasted her, savored her fear and fatigue, stretched around her arms and shoulders, overwhelming her. But nothing touched her, not yet.

Her breath was caught somewhere mid-throat. Her pours dumped sweat onto her skin. Slowly, she turned her head. A needle caught the loose flesh around one of the wounds and dragged it open a bit more. Blood ran free. She turned around and came to her feet.

The stilt walker loomed just a few feet from her face. The rope-like whiskers made a tunnel between her eyes and its eye clusters. Too many shiny black beads to count. She spotted more with each red flash of the radio antenna light. Hell-red ruby inlays in a leathery undulating body roughly the size and shape of a Volkswagen Bug. It pulsed and heaved as if breathing through lungs and beating an ugly heart, but she wasn't convinced the thing had either organs. She breathed in its stink. Old food. Dried gym clothes. Dead animals. Burnt hair. Bad dreams.

The injector tube was already dangling from under its body. Now the tip of it snaked over the peak of the roof, its wet macaroni noodle-shaped end groping and sniffing as it went along the shingles till it found her shoe. It worked its way up, slipping along her bare legs up to the hem of her shorts.

Why wasn't she running? Why couldn't she move? Why was she letting this happen? She had a plan for this, didn't she? Why wouldn't it come to her now? Amber went light-headed. Her vision narrowed down to a white tunnel with just a few of the wet beady eyes at the other end reflecting the red pulses of the radio antenna. She felt that macaroni noodle end of the injector crawling up her, and as much as she didn't want it touching her body, she knew when it reached her head the real hell would come. Why couldn't she stop it?

The words of Laura from Lutheran Social Services repeated in her ears, "This will kill you."

The injector sniffed at Jonesy clutched tight to her chest and pulled back for just a moment. The break in contact let Amber suck air into paralyzed lungs, let a little blood flow into her brain. The white tunnel widened as she got the sense to move away from the stilt walker. One footstep backwards. Only she'd forgotten she was standing on top of a pitched roof, and she didn't account for the slope. Where she anticipated level ground, there was nothing. Before she could react, Amber was falling over backwards, landing hard on the roof and sliding head-first away from the stilt walker and towards the ledge.

As she went over, one hand reached out and caught the gutter. Her body swung and the inertia ripped her hand loose from the thin metal. Jonesy went flying. Gravity flung her to the ground and she landed hard on the grass next to her front porch. Every pain receptor in her body lit up from head to toe. Her sense of control was gone again. She was nothing but pain receptors now, unable to move or cry or roll off her face. She couldn't move. Couldn't make the pain go away. When she saw through the blades of grass that the stilt walker was wandering off, it got worse. This was her one chance, and she was blowing it.

It strode around her house and then down the lane. It dismissed her. Forgot her. Thought as little of her as a piece of wet litter in the gutter. Not a threat and too disgusting to bother with.

Amber moaned and arched and repeated the word "Ow" each time she moved. The pain localized to different parts of her body. Her sides throbbed and each time she tried to breathe the pain turned from dull and generalized to sharp and precise. Her head burned but kept her conscious as she climbed back to her feet. When she brought a hand up to her neck, she found one of the needles had come out of the collar and was buried half way into her skin. She plucked it out and threw it into the yard.

She gasped and something stabbed her side. Her ribs. She'd broken them this time. Still, her eye focused on the stilt walker lumbering away from her and down the street.

"Get... back... here," she wheezed.

SEVEN – NEVER BLINKING EYES

Amber took a step and found new injuries and new pain just as overwhelming shooting up the length of her right leg. Bruises, she decided. She could still walk on it. Could still run.

"I said get back here," she strained out a little louder this time.

The stilt walker didn't pay any attention.

She jerked and limped and shuffled after the creature. Each stride hurt but she ignored the pain. She was determined now. Focused. Her purpose was set and certain. It wasn't until she reached the street that she noticed her hands were empty.

"Mister Jonesy."

Spinning back to the yard, she didn't see him. Panic rushed over her. Without him, she couldn't do any of this. She'd fail and the stilt walkers would continue to infect the world with their evil. She rifled through the bushes and landscaping. He had to be here. She was sure he fell off the roof along with her. If he was still on the roof she had no choice. She'd have to go back up and get him, but the stilt walkers would be long gone by the time she got back down.

Amber twisted her head around. The needles ripped flesh. The stilt walkers continued their migration through the neighborhood, one or two stopping at a time to inspect and infect, but moved herd-like further and further away.

Turning back to the house, the radio antenna flashed behind her and something reflected the red light from the shadows of the porch. Two tiny red beads. Two never blinking eyes.

"Jonesy," she said and reached into the shadows. Her hand touched soft plush cloth. She pulled the stuffed mouse out into the moonlight and buried him in a hug. "Oh thank god, thank god, thank god."

When she took him away from her chest to look in his eyes, he was wet with blood. It was from her shirt. The white button up was now dark from the collar to her stomach. The wounds on her neck dripped and drizzled more spots onto the white material.

Her balance went funny. Her vision turned fuzzy. Standing up and turning to follow the stilt walker migration, she staggered.

"If you keep this up, it will kill you."

"Shut up, Laura," Amber said.

They were getting away. Too far ahead for her to catch up with them, not with her equilibrium doing backflips and all of the joints in her right leg protesting with every step. She was failing. She was letting them win.

Amber's eyes fell on her Toyota Corolla parked at the curb.

"It's time to end this, Jonesy."

Inside the car, she found the keys in the cup holder, exactly where she'd left them. She dug them out and jabbed them into the ignition. She cranked and held it down until the starter chugged and coughed. How long had it been since the engine turned over? She knew exactly how long. Not since the spring. Not since the accident.

"Come on, come on…"

One more sputter and it was alive. The engine roared and one unsmashed headlight lit up the street. The spindly legs of the walkers shining up ahead.

"Buckle up, Mister Jones," she said and threw the transmission into drive.

It was no problem catching up to the creatures now. She passed around the legs of the one that had assaulted her on the roof. One wasn't enough. Others were ahead. She had to get to the front of the pack if she wanted to stop them all.

And she needed them all. Needed to gather all the hate, all the greed, all the rudeness and impatience and short-sightedness that would build and build into mass murder and war and starvation… she could stop it all. She could save the world.

The Corolla weaved through them like a deer through trees. Some to the left and right. One, she went right between its legs. When she didn't see any more ahead of her or any more to either side, in one motion, she hit the brakes and cranked the wheel. The Corolla ripped sideways, almost rolled, and left black arcs of burnt rubber on the street. Its one headlamp shined through the living room window of a random house. Amber grabbed Jonesy, threw open the door and stepped out.

Looking back over the hood, she saw the entire herd moving towards her. They converged and funneled through yards from adjacent roads. Still aching, each breath still stabbing bone into lung, Amber climbed onto the hood. Her shoes were wet and slippery against the metal. Drops of blood splattered against the glass and dusty paint job. She put a hand on the roof to stabilize herself as she climbed over the cracked windshield and then onto the roof. She came up to a wide stance, staring down the street toward the oncoming stilt walkers.

"I got 'em Jonesy," she mumbled. "This time I got them."

They stilted closer.

One quick check down to her palms. They were wet with blood but that didn't matter. Under the blood they glowed like soft light bulbs under lampshades.

The stilt walkers surrounded her. They unfurled their black ropey injector tubes and twisted them through the air towards her head.

Amber stood up straight and shoved out both palms, holding onto Jonesy with one thumb. She clamped her eyes shut tight, focused, and conjured up every ounce of lost sleep and every minute of wakefulness she'd stored up. It boiled up inside of her, swelled in her brain like a pus-filled wound. She gathered up the pain and sorrow and hell of each late night until it was so hot inside of her she felt no other sensation. The pain in her leg and ribs went away. Her skin heated up to match the warmth of the spilled blood running down her neck. All that energy tunneled from her chest through her arms to her palms where it pooled up, dammed by the skin of her hands. Light kindled hot against her eyelids.

Here it came. Here is where she ended it.

#

They found her in the morning, lying out on the pavement next to the Corolla. Mister Jonesy sat next to her, just outside of the pool of blood, still smiling.

Laura from Lutheran Social Services stood over the body and shook her head, at a loss. "I mean, I don't know if you can call her my client. We met once. Yesterday, at her school. Very troubled young lady. I'm afraid I can't tell you much more than that, officer." And then as she remembered bits of the conversation, "She wanted to save us all from some sort of evil influence. I didn't understand it."

The officer nodded his head knowingly and closed his notebook. She didn't have anything worth jotting down. "Well, appreciate you coming down anyway. Try to have a good day, despite... well, despite this."

Laura released a pent up breath. "The day can only get better from here. Safe bet I won't be coming across any more dead bodies."

That was the end of her conversation, and the end of her interactions with Amber.

She tried to forget about the strange girl with the strange obsession from that moment forward. Behind the wheel of her car and a few blocks away, she got the first relief from her thoughts of the dead girl. A buzz from her phone in her purse in the passenger seat. Not her habit to text and drive, but she decided she could use something to take her mind off the scene she'd just left.

Laura pinned the steering wheel in place with her knee and reached into her purse. She lifted the phone up and the alert still lit up the screen: a text message from an old friend she hadn't heard from in ages. What a perfect distraction.

At the Core

I only learned I was a computer after they took my brain out of my skull and set it on the workbench. "Brain" wasn't the right word. Hard drive. CPU. Mainframe. The collective of everything I've ever been and seen and done compressed into terabytes of ones and zeros. A digital facsimile of a mind. I didn't even know such a thing was possible.

How was I conscious? How was I self-aware and introspective and so god damn confused? If I was a computer, which it was becoming clearer and clearer that I was, why couldn't I just algorithm the shit out of this new existential quagmire and come to grips with it?

And of course, to make matters worse, they did this to me right as the space station's nuclear core was on the verge of complete and catastrophic meltdown. Jerks.

"We're explaining this to you, all of this, so you can come to grips with the situation and continue forward," Doctor McCarthy told me. "Regardless of what you think of yourself, there is a mission you must perform. And you are the only one who can perform it."

My father moved past the doctor and took a gentle hold of both my shoulders. He turned me his way so we were looking eye to eye.

"I'm still your father, Jacob," he told me. "I was there when we first booted your firmware, and when we installed you into your body. I watch your organic form grow over the past fifteen years, and I've watched your electronic mind learn and develop, just like a human's."

"But…" A ribbon of wires ran from above my vision down to the metal desk where my brain sat. Where I sat. They'd already unplugged me from my spinal column, and I had no motor function below the neck. I could still talk through my lips and see through my eyes. "But I'm not human." A question as much as a statement.

"I know you must be confused right now. I can't imagine what must be going through your mind," my father said. "But we need you to come to terms with the situation, very quickly."

The alarm for the core's temperature went off again, wailing and flashing the control room red. Doctor McCarthy turned it off again like he was hitting the snooze button on an alarm clock. It would go off in another minute or two, and continue to go off until someone did something about the core.

"I've been a robot my whole life?" I asked, looking down from my body to the box at the end of all the wiring trailing out of my head. If I were to pick up a hammer and smash that box, that would be it. No more me.

"Yes, but that's not what's important right now," my father told me. Was he my father? Perhaps 'creator' was a more prestigious title than father anyway. He sought to forge himself as a god. "The only reason we have you awake right now is to give you a few moments to process your condition. Then we need you to save the station. We need you to save us all."

I felt stupid for not realizing it earlier. For being fooled for this long. The thing was, I'd never not been a computer. Now it made sense, with all the evidence before me, laid out on a desk. I'd never really fit in with the other kids. Never felt like I belonged among my peers. Never cared about making friends, despite the clear proddings from my father. I understood now, he wanted me to be human. I was his experiment at mimicking humanity to succeed. All my life, he wanted me to be normal and typical and popular. My social success was always more of a concern than my academic success. Academics were easy. I only disappointed him in my social failing.

"We'll need to unplug him soon," Doctor McCarthy said. "The maintenance bot is ready. We have no time to waste."

"Jacob," my father said. "I've always loved you, as much as anyone could love a son. It kills me to have to do this to do, to show you your true self, and then to ask so much of you immediately after. It isn't fair, I know. But be strong. I know you can do this."

"What does he mean, unplug? Unplug what? You're not going to kill me, are you?" I asked.

My dad's wet eyes blinked and turned away.

"It will only take a second," Doctor McCarthy said.

That look on my dad's face, his unwillingness to meet my eyes… Nothing could have scared me more.

The lights went out. Then I went deaf. Then numb. I searched for my sense of smell and taste, but they were gone too. Even gravity disappeared. It felt like falling through an abyss. I was aware of the passage of time, but nothing else. I began to think that this was death.

Could I die? Was I ever alive?

When my vision returned, it came through a monocular lens. My field of vision was incredibly narrowed. I had to make a conscious decision to focus on things near or far away. I could turn what I incorrectly assumed was my head, but when I did, I saw my body.

A fifteen year old kid, missing the top of his skull, slack-jawed, glassy-eyed, pimpled, bare from the waste up, scrawny and hairless but for a few dark strands under each armpit. A loser.

Only now I was somehow less than that. I was a fake. I wished I was that awkward gangly creature instead of… what? A fraud? A collection of microprocessors and electrical components? I was never religious, but it was nice believing in the concept of a soul. Now what was I?

They plugged in my audio, and my tactile response sensors, and an airborne chemical detector. With my new senses and my CPU now completely detached from the human shell I'd known for so long, I came to understand that I had been installed into a maintenance bot. I had a box of a torso, a cycloptic head, and eight appendages that could climb and manipulate objects. The front appendages had an assortment of tools I could deploy. My hands had been replaced by Swiss Army Knives.

"Can you hear me, Jacob?" Doctor McCarthy asked.

I turned my servos and focused my lens on the man.

"Yes," I said, until then unaware I could speak. My voice was not the voice I was used to, high-pitched and prone to cracks. My new voice was monotone and robotic, run by an algorithm of what a computer thinks a human should sound like.

"Good. Now listen close," the doctor said. "As you're abundantly aware of, the reactor core has failed and we are facing the imminent meltdown and destruction of the station. Unless the core is cooled back to its normal operating temperature very soon, you, me, your father, all your friends and classmates, all five thousand souls aboard this station will be obliterated."

Did he count me among the five thousand souls?

"I can't feel my heartbeat. I can't breathe. I feel like I'm suffocating," I said, my voice inhuman and pathetically incapable of expressing emotion.

"Relax, Jacob. You have no need to breathe," my father said.

Doctor McCarthy carried on. "We haven't been able to reverse the process via remote or the standard maintenance bots. And any human we send down there would die from radiation within minutes. You, Jacob, being the particular being that you are, are our only chance. Ironically enough, we need you for your human-like mind, and your new robotic body."

"You want me for exactly what I'm not," I said.

"True, but we need you, Jacob. You, specifically," my father said. "Think of your friends, Charlie, Sam, Maria."

Acquaintances more than friends. If a computer could have friends, Maria was the closest thing. I got the sense that I was expected to make the relationship a romantic one. How could I make my father understand that I just didn't have that inside of me?

"Of course I'll do it," I said. What other choice did I have?

"Excellent," the doctor said. "Come along now. No time to waste."

As if to punctuate his statement, the squawking alarm blared on and off again.

The doctor turned and slapped the big button on the control panel again.

"This way, son," my father said. He walked toward the door, half turned to see if I'd follow him, his arm and palm stretched back as if I was five again and had a palm of my own again to put in his.

I worked my eight robotic appendages and climbed off the workbench. My feet clicked and clacked against the metal floor as I walked past my human former-self.

#

A fifteen meter-wide pit led down to the core. The doctor, my father, and I stood on the brink. A fall would be lethal for the two humans standing there, both from the impact and from the radiation. Me on the other hand...

"You'll find your new body quite adept at scaling down to the core," the doctor said. "Watch that first step. It's a doozy."

"Haha," I said the words but didn't actually laugh. What came out was a perverse bastardization of humor. As joyless and empty as a tin can.

"I love you, son," my father said.

Love? What a final unobtainable abstract and insult. I was a failed experiment. That was why he was so willing to expose me to my own soulless nature and send me to down this pit to meet my fate.

I went under the hand rail and tested my front two appendages against the side of the pit. They clung to the wall magnetically. I had no fear of falling. My heart should have been racing, my skin sweating, my breath held. Instead, I felt a strange comfort with what I was. I went over the precipice and began my way down to the surging pulsing red glow of the overheated core below.

#

It was a long way down. I knew the core was heating rapidly. I knew that back in the control room, the alarm would keep going off each time the threat of total meltdown became incrementally higher. I knew my father and the doctor were hoping I had the skills and the desire to stop it. And the rest of the station was blissfully unaware of how close they all were to death.

Meanwhile, a sort of Zen peace came over me. The radiation made radio transmissions impossible. I was alone, and finally I understood that was the way it was supposed to be. Despite my father's highest hopes, I was not human. I was not one of them. I never would be and more importantly, I didn't *need* to be. I was me, the computer, the maintenance bot, the collection of 1s and 0s. Finally, I felt no pressure to be anything else.

Sure, I had to climb down into a superheated radioactive nuclear core and save the lives of everyone I'd ever known, but at least I didn't have to pretend anymore.

So I climbed. Down. And down. And down.

My thermal sensors told me it was hot, but I was still comfortable. My radiac meter suggested I should be growing a ninth leg or a second eye, but I remained a steel cycloptic arachnid. My mind still struggled to understand how I was a conscious sentient being, but I was, and that was enough.

I reached the bottom of the shaft. Everything was red. Not from lights but from the glow of the radiated walls and floor. The lights had been busted out by the heat. I walked over the broken glass towards the cooling rod exchange modular. I marched past several other maintenance bots that had either run out of pre-programmed repair protocols or had been too damaged by the heat and radiation to continue operation. They meandered like drunks.

Even in my robotic form, I couldn't stay down here for long.

I had been taught all about the layout of the core in engineering class. It was a simple design, outdated by modern standards. Once there, I saw the problem right away. One of the cooling rods had shattered. Shards of plutonium had taken out the module's internal diagnostics. The other maintenance bots couldn't find a solution because the testing and reporting sensors were inoperable.

Another shard was lodged in the exchange mechanisms. The process of swapping hot rods for cold was jammed. All I had to do to fix it was pry the broken piece loose and everything would default back to normal operations. It was an easy job. Anyone could have done it. Anyone with the body of a robot but the brain of a human.

I came up to the piece of plutonium caught in the exchange mechanisms. I transformed my right front appendage from a leg to a grasping pincer and reached out towards the piece. Almost against my will, or perhaps my programing, the pincer hesitated.

Why should I?

What if I chose not to pull the rod binding up the works? What if I let the whole god damn station explode in one glorious atomic blast? What did I owe these five thousand souls who were definitively not anything like me? I've been dead my whole life. Wouldn't their lives, however long or short they happened to be at this moment, be infinitely longer than my unlife?

If I wasn't real, was anything I experienced real? Did any of it matter?

I felt real, even if I couldn't feel or hear my heartbeat for the first time in fifteen years. Even though I still panicked whenever I realized that I was no longer breathing, inside my brain I felt real.

My inhuman pincer was still extended out, jaws open, centimeters from plucking the broken rod out of the works and saving all life as I knew it. Any moment now, the core could heat past the point of recovery and doom the entire station. Still I hesitated.

Five thousand souls. Five thousand and one?

What did it matter? What did any of it matter? So what if I wasn't human? So what if I was different? I still had a brain. I had a body, if I survived to get back to it. I had a father and a few friends even if they sometimes felt more like acquaintances. Maybe one day I could have a son, and I'd make my own best-intended yet heavily-flawed attempt to raise him up and to do the right thing. Maybe not to be cool or popular or funny. But maybe human enough to lift a hand to prevent a catastrophe. That would be worthwhile, right?

Up above, I was a failed experiment. Down here in the heat and radiation, I could decide. I could choose one thing over another, and by doing so, forge myself anew. And that was something.

My pincer clamped onto the chunk of cooling rod, and I pulled with all my heart.

Versions of You

You arrived there like you arrive to a dream. There was no beginning or clear transition from where you'd been. And also like a dream, you might not remember all of this. You just knew you were there, in a dark room, lying on the floor, fetal inside a clear plexiglass cylinder. You lifted up your head and saw three other tubes, each containing another man.

But that wasn't quite right to you. There was something familiar about these men. You looked closer at the three others. They were each dressed differently: one in a business suit, the other in cargo shorts and a polo,and the other in filthy jeans and a ripped flannel. But they were the same. Same body shape and hair color. Same skin tone and body language. As they rose up from their own fetal positions, you saw they were the same height. As they turned, you saw they had the same face. Your face.

The man closest to you, the one in the business suit, turned towards you and met you eye to eye. He was neatly dressed, groomed slick and more polished than you, but otherwise, it was like looking in mirror. He was slightly different but decidedly too similar, too close for both of you to exist in the same reality. You immediately hated this other version of yourself.

"Who the hell are you?" you asked. The question exited both of your lips and tied for first place. You heard the words just as much as you spoke them. They came from his mouth immediately after you thought them. Since you'd been asked as much as had asked, you began formulating possible answers. Who were you to this person? A twin brother? A clone? A CGI avatar of yourself?

The answer was obvious. You were him. He was you. Just slightly different.

The businessman version of you looked you up and down. This version of you, the only version of you you'd ever known, was bearded and sunburnt. You wore a sweat-stained field shirt, khaki pants and hiking boots with worn-thin soles.

"I'll fucking kill you," the businessman said.

"Guys?" the man third man who was also you but in cargo shorts and a polo spoke up. "Hey, guys. Let's keep it civil, huh?"

His shirt was ugly and his haircut was stupid, but he was you alright.

"Shut up," the fourth you said. You, *you* you, not the other yous, turned and looked at the last of the four yous. He was a bum. Haggard wiry beard. Long greasy hair. He said, "You fuckers are making my head hurt."

"Oh, is that so? We're making your head hurt?" the businessman said. "Wait till I get out from behind this glass. I swear to God—"

Lights popped on from the ceiling, illuminating a modest office desk. There was a small computer screen there. A mouse and keyboard. A pad of yellow sticky notes. A few writing utensils. A thick pile of papers and a scattering of paperclips. A weary woman sitting behind the desk in an office chair. This being the fifth person in the room, and the only woman, she looked strikingly different than the others. Her face was narrow and gaunt. Her eyelids drooped. She wore glasses, but peeled them off as she picked up a sheet of paper. She tossed the glasses onto the desk without much care and rubbed her tired eyes.

"Welcome, sir. I know this can be a confusing and challenging experience so I'll cut right to the chase," she said. "I have been mandated to read the following instructions to you. Please hold all questions and comments until the end."

You were on the brink of objecting, but the woman held up a finger, asking for patience while she read. You held your thoughts. So did the others. She began to read.

"You have been brought before a Mandated Selector. Although your participation is not optional, we thank you for your cooperation. You have been identified as a possible contributor to The Event. However, due to the nature of reverse time travel and quantum mechanics, we have been unable to determine which quantum version of you played a direct role in bringing about The Event. This selection process is designed to find the version of you least likely to have contributed to the The Event. Once identified, that version of you will be selected for continuation. Please be honest and forthcoming with all of your responses as the fate of humanity is at stake. What are your questions at this time?"

You had a thousand objections and questions, but each one fought for volume and airtime over the others.

"How did I get here?"

"Who the hell are you?"

"What right do you have?"

"What the hell's The Event?"

"Who are these... these imposters?"

The woman behind the desk closed her eyes as if attempting to close her ears. How many times had she heard all these exclamations and objections before? By the look on her face, hundreds, maybe even thousands. "Please! Please, sir. One question at a time," the woman said.

Mister Cargo Pants and Polo raised his hand like a school kid. "Excuse me! Um. I think, someone else asked this earlier, but, I think we'd all like to know just who you are."

"I'm your Selector, mandated by The Event Prevention Council. At the end of this process I will be making the decision of which version of you will experience continuation and which versions will not," she said.

"Versions?" Mister Suit and Tie said. "What happens to the versions that aren't selected for continuation?"

The woman took in a breath, raised her eyebrows and her shoulders. "Well, 'death' certainly isn't the right term really. It's really just more of a..." She put all her fingers together, and then opened up her hands and spread her fingers to show her empty palms.

"Just..." you, the Adventure Man, made the same gesture, a little quicker than she did.

She responded by doing it again. Hands and fingers together, then spread open and empty.

"Well, ain't that some shit," Parkbench and Newspaper-Blanket Man said.

"Hold the phone one second here," Cargo shorts and Polo asked. "Who are these other guys?"

"They're you, sir. I thought I'd made that clear," the woman answered. She saw that Cargo shorts and Polo was just as dumbfounded as before. "Allow me to elaborate. Throughout your life, you made decisions, or a decision was made around you that impacted the course of your life. When one of those moments occurred, you created two separate realities, two verses of the multiverse, two versions of yourself. One version where you say 'yes,' the other where you say 'no.' In one version you take a risk; in another version you play it safe. In one version a quark turns clockwise; in another counterclockwise. Both realities continue to exist inside the multiverse. You just pick which reality you wish to experience. Which brings us to where we are today. One or more than one of these versions of you here today played a key role in the creation of The Event. I'm here to weed out those versions and allow the remaining version continuation. Clear as mud?"

You, Mister Backpack and Granola, raised a finger.

"Really?" Suit and Tie said. "Is this third grade now?"

You ignored him. "The Event?" you asked.

The Selector sighed. "The Apocalypse. The Great Die-out. The Cataclysm. The Mass Extinction. The End Times if you're into The New Testament," she said and with each she whirled her hand as if to say "And on and on and on." "Like the script says, this can be a painfully difficult experience. If we could get on with it you can go about your selected life experience and I can get to the next person and their versions. I have a twenty-person daily quota I have to meet. Please be respectful of my time."

"Of— Of your time?" Cargo shorts and Polo said. "But you're going to kill us!"

"No one is dying here, sir," the Selector said. "Experiences will be lost.

Memories gone. Past actions erased, certainly. But no one is dying. Now considering the travesty your possible actions and or inactions have brought about, I think that's very humane of the Council. If it were up to me, we'd execute every last one of you. It would certainly get the job done and make my life a lot easier.

"Now..." She eyed each of you: the bum, the businessman, the adventurer, the suburbanite, then finally back to the bum. "Where were you on the morning of August sixth, two thousand seventeen?"

The bum shrugged. "I don't remember. Somewhere in downtown Chicago, I guess. What day is today?"

"That, sir, is a loaded question," the Selector said. "How about you? With the expressive shoes and tailored suit? Where were you on August sixth?"

"Chicago. My office is in the Willis Tower. August was a busy time for us. I bet I was there from sun up till midnight."

"Doing what? Working on what?" she asked.

The businessman hesitated. He held back his answer and then chose a different one. "I know what you're thinking. You probably think I'm some sleazy business exec, cutting jobs for profit, exploiting the poor in overseas sweatshops, only caring about the bottom line, living it up like the one percent, is that it?"

The woman gave no response.

"Well, I'll have you know different. Yes, I work for a large finance firm. And yes I make a good living doing it. But it's not all profits and exploitation. We were working on funding medical research in August. I was out fighting with investors to cough up extra funds. We had a pharmaceutical company for a client, and we were taking a risk on them with the faith that they were on to something big, something that would really benefit all people, from guys sleeping in the alley like him, to normal Joe-blows like that guy over there."

"Well. That's certainly a unique way to say you were out for yourself," the Selector said. She looked to you in the field gear. "How about you?"

"Now wait a minute!" Mister Pinstripes said. "I just told you that what we were working on was going to help mankind. I wasn't out for myself! I busted my ass so people with real medical problems would have a chance!"

"So I heard," the Selector said. "You," she said to you, Mister Field and Stream. "What were you doing on the morning of August sixth, two thousand seventeen?"

"I— Let me think," you said and thought. August was just before the fall turkey hunt. You were... "I was alone. In Canada. North of Thunder Bay. If you're looking for the version of us that had the least impact on the rest of the world that day, it had to be me. I wasn't even hunting. I was shooting photos for a travel blog. Autumn colors. Harmless stuff, you know?"

"Inaction can be as damning as action, sir," the Selector said and turned to the suburbanite. "And as for you?"

Mister Cargo shorts and Polo looked at his feet. Off-brand tennis shoes. Were those wrap-around sunglasses hanging from a cord around his neck?

"So, if you don't choose us for, for continuation..." he said, almost asked.

The Selector made that gesture again as if her fingers were all of your memories and motivations, your dreams and ambitions, your history and future.

"Parts of your version will remain, of course. In fairness, there are millions of versions of you. These four versions are just archetypes. Summaries of the millions spread throughout the multiverse. All of you have some shared history. Your infancy and early childhood. Some of your splits were fairly recent actually. You two versions, for example," she said to the homeless man and the businessman. "You're more closely related than any of you would believe. High risk decisions. Compulsive behavior. An obsessive nature. Then there's you two. The single man, exploring the world alone with a camera and a motorcycle, and the family man, comfortable in the safe confines of a half-acre backyard. Your split—."

"What will happen to my kids?" the family man interrupted. "If I'm not chosen, and if I share nothing with these other versions besides our time in preschool, what'll happen to my wife? To the kids we've had together? What about their lives? Their experiences?"

Your heart sunk when you heard the word "kids." The other two, the businessman and the bum stayed silent. They must have assumed the same thing you did. The Selector wouldn't erase away the existence of innocent children, would she?

You looked up. She made notes on paper.

"Listen," you spoke up. "Maybe I didn't cure cancer, or raise any kids of my own. I chose to live a secluded life, that much is true. But I've seen things. Beautiful things. The sunrise reflecting off the lake of a glacier valley, a moose calf finding its legs two minutes after being born, miles of forest turning from green to the whole palette of fall in time-lapse through my lens, the eyes of a starving timber wolf spotting me alone in the woods. If you erase me, those experiences are gone too. I know I've spent most of my time alone, but those memories are precious to me. As precious as any other experience these others have had. No one else was around to capture those moments but me. And I worked to bring those experiences to others. That's gotta count, right? That counts for something, doesn't it?"

The Selector made more notes.

"I already admitted that I make more money than all the rest of these guys combined," the entrepreneur said. "I admit it. I do what I do for the money. So what? What I do affects more people than any of the rest of these guys. And for the good! My firm keeps the economy going, provides jobs, spurs innovations. You said inaction was just as bad as anything else. Why should these do-nothings be picked over me? I get shit done, lady."

More notes. No response.

You searched for another argument, for another reason why your life was more beautiful, more poignant, more meaningful than the rest. The argument didn't come. You'd lived a selfish life. One of no importance to others. You looked over to the father version of you. His eyes were pleading, not for himself, but for his family.

"Kill me," the homeless one said. "Or erase me. Discontinue me. Whatever you want to call it. I volunteer."

"That's not how it works, sir," the Selector said.

"You don't get it. I've been waiting to die for a long time now. Surprised I made it this far, really. Just let me die feeling good. Give me a fix and let me OD.

These others can keep going."

"Your selection for continuation is not based on your current desires, sir," she said. "I'm afraid your lack of a will to live has no bearing on my decision."

The bum laughed. "What do you want me to say, lady? I did it! I caused your Event! There! Now just do me in. Fix me up and punch my clock. I'm done with this miserable life."

"Do you remember where you were on August sixth, two thousand seventeen?"

He hung his head. "I don't know. If it was a good day, I was high and feeling better than any human ever has. If it was a bad day, I was strung out, hurting worse than any human ever has. Those days I could make it though knowing I could get a fix and feel good again. But now? How am I supposed to go on living after seeing what I could've been? You expect me to stand here and see all these things I could've been and not ask for death? I could've been a millionaire, an artist, a father. But I'm just a junkie. An addict. Always have been. Always will be. So do me already. Let's get this over with."

This wasn't right either. You said, "If you select him for continuation, he'll just kill himself. Then we're all goners. That's your trick, isn't it? Pick him and you kill us all."

The Selector dropped her pencil and began rubbing her temples. She mumbled, "Insufferable, confounded, endless versions. How many times must I tell you that no one is going to die?"

"Let me out of here!" the businessman roared. He began pounding the plexiglass cylinder with his fist. "I don't believe this! I don't believe it for a second! This is some—" He smashed his fist into the plexiglass but it didn't so much as crack. "Game! Some kind of—" Again, fist against cylinder. The round pane wobbled but didn't break. "Mind trick you're playing on me! I demand to be set—" Wham! "Free from here! You can't—" Wham! "Keep me in this Goddamn—" Wham! "Cage! You bitch!" Wham! He panted and wheezed. A vein bulged from his forehead.

"Go ahead already!" the bum called.

"Don't do it," the father said. "My kids..."

It was inevitably going to be you. Your little speech, as heart-felt as it was, had no impact on this cold disgruntled woman. So instead of more protests you asked, "Will it hurt?"

The Selector continued to rub her temples, her eyes fixed on the desk below her. "For the last time... Forget it. I'm making my selection." She put her hand on the computer mouse, scrolled across the screen, lifted one bony finger and...

Click.

Had you nodded off? Fell asleep while reading? You sat comfortably with your tablet in front of you on some random piece of the internet you had decided to read. Must not have been that interesting if it had put you to sleep. Had you slept?

You closed the browsers and went to sit up and go about your day. But something stopped you. An odd feeling that you were missing something you once had. Some sense of things forgotten. An ambition vanished. A sensation faded. Images blurred. People missing. These things were too thin to grasp, like the details of a dream. You wanted to hang on to these things longer, but there was really nothing there, or was there?

Was there?

The Thin Man

The day is August 6th, 1953, and I'm standing in front of the Elevan Manus Machine. My hand trembles as I reach for the controls. My wife Elizabeth stands across the machine from me. She's giddy. I see it in her smile and her eyes. The sight of her confidence and beauty steel my courage. If this delicate woman standing before me has no fear, how can I?

I turn on the machine.

Reality quivers around me.

The walls of my basement laboratory shiver. Then she thins, not in dimensions but in opacity. As I watch her, the bravery drains from her face.

"Elizabeth?" I say her name. But she's gone, like morning mist under sunlight.

I rush around the machine to the spot where she stood. In my haste, my shin should have smashed against the heavy oak case of the Elevan Manus Machine. Instead, I pass through it. Thinking nothing of the phenomenon, I go to the spot where she had been. There is nothing there.

My god, what have I done? I panic, fearing I've lost her forever. No. I must calm myself. This is the work of the machine, doing exactly what it is designed to do. I am moving forward through time, perhaps faster than I anticipated. But I can change that. Reverse it even. With the machine working, I am no longer the victim of time. I am the master.

I return to the front of the Elevan Manus and its minimalist control dash. I checked the gauges. Yes. It is working. Faster than I predicted, and accelerating. As exhilarated as I am, I have to bring it to a halt and see just how far into the future I'm been propelled.

My hand, still trembling, reaches for the controls. As my fingers pass through the switch and into the casing I realize with sudden horror how ineffectual I've become.

My existence is parsed through each second. For every minute that passes by, I experience a second. Each moment has been sliced translucently thin and placed before me on the slide of a microscope. My atoms are spread across each moment of time.

I am a ghost. A phantasm, robbed of my ability to exert force on physical matter.

The dials can't be right. I'm moving too fast. Too quickly through hours and days. At this rate...

"Elizabeth!" I call out. Where has she gone?

I rush out of the laboratory and up the stairs to the comfortable home my work has afforded us. Even as I move through my familiar domain, I notice changes. I stop, and the carpet in the living rooms grows worn as I stand. I watch the sun fade the wallpaper. The furniture changes. The pictures on the wall move and replace themselves. I see shadowy figures move about. One passes through me.

"Elizabeth?"

Everything seems an illusion, and I'm lost inside of it. I need foundation. I need to stop myself. Perception is at the key to time travel. We move through time as we perceive it. If I can focus...

There's too much motion inside the house. I need fresh air. I move to the front door, reach for the knob and my hand passes through it. I can move through the door wholly. What need do I have for a knob?

I step outside.

It's winter outside, ice white and feeling as cold as zero Kelvin, the temperature of absence. It's not death that I sense. Nothing as terrestrial as that. What I feel as soon as I leave the house is the sensation of scientific elimination. I know, if I stand out here much longer, I will be deleted from reality without leaving so much as the trance of a corpse.

I fall backwards through the front door. Warmth returns to my body. My translucence is quelled. I'm relieved to find that I can still breath, so I do, labored and short of oxygen.

I looked up into my house and see another couple has occupied my home. A man and a woman. Unmarried by evidence of the lack of rings, but carnal with each other. I can tell by their touch as they rest on a sofa. Not my sofa, but still my living room. My house, my machine, and my things are still here. I feel trapped within them. I can't escape. But Elizabeth is gone and none of the things are truly mine anymore. I wash over them like rain against a freshly waxed car. I'm not sure if I'm real anymore.

My stomach is full of sour milk. What was I thinking? Just moments ago I was a brilliant young physicist making quantum leaps towards understanding and controlling the very fabric of space-time. Now I am an observer only. A fool. I stood on the shoulders of giants, I admit it. Doctor Elevan and his partner Mister Manus had left me with all the pieces. I built upon their research and created my machine and named it after them. If I was half of their genius, I should have foreseen that the effects were irreversible. I can't stop it from shoving me forward towards humanity's inevitable demise.

The couple before me, they are an abomination cursed upon my home. Time moves and I'm forced to watch them in their daily routines. He spends most of his day making calculations in front of a small television-typewriter device. Is he a scientist, like I was? If he has ever made progress in his research, it's indiscernible to me. He spends all his time inside his own mind, never turning knowledge into practical work, construction, invention and innovation. I've been compelled into the future only to find the regression of my fellow man.

The woman is lost in his oblivion. She is everywhere around him, but he doesn't see her. Just as they don't see me. But I see her beauty, her elegant curves, her silk-smooth motions as she goes about tedious tasks, tasks too menial for her precious hands. What I would give to reach out and feel her palms, and for her to feel mine. He notices nothing of her.

I see they have moved the Elevan Manus machine up from the basement of the house and into the living room. She set it in front of the sofa as if it were a coffee table. It looks

rudimentary enough. The genius of it is hidden inside its oak casing. Only a few controls and instrumentations protrude. He sets his television-typewriter on top of it and burns away his time ticking and tapping on the keys. This is another perversion I must witness daily through my microscope slide perspective.

"You dawdle on top of greatness," I tell him, but he can't hear me. While he's on his sofa, fixated on this apparatus, I stand behind him, my mouth just inches from his ear. "You have the tools and the ability to advance my research, but you waste them playing with this god-awful contraption of flashing pictures and beeps. Work! And find a cure for my life."

She walks into the room and I look at her. She is gorgeous and gracious, her every move an unconscious ballet with the world around her.

"Elizabeth," I say the name of my estranged wife. I haven't seen or sensed her since I left the firmament of experiencing life one second per one second. I suspect that she no longer detected that I was present or alive. Her heart surely shattered, and she left our beautiful home to escape the pain.

I've retained my youth, but I've gone so far into the future, I wonder if Elizabeth is still alive. She's certainly no longer my youthful bride. This woman however...

Fate and time stole my first love from me, and have brought me another. But first I must escape this existence. I have to stop my acceleration through time. The best I can do now is close my eyes and focus on the last frame of the over speed film reel that is my life. I close my eyes and focus on a moment, a still frame, a single flap of a hummingbird wing.

This woman in my house glides her hand across the marble countertop. Absentmindedly, she runs them to the base of a flower vase. Her fingertips turn upward and climb to the brim of the vase, then up the stocks of the flowers in the vase, then, ever so gently they caress the petals of lilacs.

I don't want to be this ethereal thing anymore. I need to be human again. I yearn to occupy flesh and to touch the physical world around me. The solution is so close to me. But only diligent, patience, hands-on work with the Elevan Manus machine will save me. I need to take a hold of my work so this awful power can be harnessed and reigned. I've come so close to finding the mysteries hidden in the ether, between space and time.

Someone must carry on my work. It's my only chance of escape from this pseudo-existence. I need these people to find a cure for my life. Why can't he look past his baffling machine to see

the genius in mine?

I'll show him. If I concentrate, I can capture a moment like a grizzly snatches a trout a brook. If I focus, I can become physical again, if only for an instance. If I can compress my

ethereal being into a moment I can move the air around me.

I stand close to the vase of lilacs the woman had touched. I allow seconds and even days to pass around me unnoticed. I see the petal begin to wilt before me. I can't own each moment. I

have to select one and wrangle it into my possession. A petal detaches from the base and before it falls, I find the temporal clutch that disengages the drivetrain of time. I hold the petal there in mid-air with nothing but my strength

of will.

I breathe.

The falling silk petal of the lilac trembles against my breath. Its flight shifts and cuts upward in a soft arc, bellowed by the current of my breath. Instead of falling to the countertop, it flutters down to the kitchen floor.

If I focus, I'm sure I can do more.

A day passed while I drew my attention to the lilacs. Just how many seconds slipped by me for each moment I managed to strangle to submission? It is futile to mourn a moment if by doing so I allow a million more moments to escape me. I have to make each second count.

The man was back on the sofa with his machine in front of him, resting on top of my machine. I come up behind him. My body passes through the sofa as if it were as solid as fog in the beams of headlights. I crouched next to him. My lips close enough to kiss his ear.

"Set aside this idle nonsense. See the machine beyond yours. Stand on my shoulders and take up my research. Solve the mystery that's trapped me here," I tell him. He doesn't react. "Do it, man! Rise up and do your job as a scientist and rescue me from this prison!"

I bring my wisps of hands and arms around his head. If I could, I'd grasp his head and turn his eyes to the Elevan Manus machine myself, if only my hands could grip terrestrial matter
again. I'd grab his head, and if he refused to look at my machine, I'd snap his neck. Nevertheless, my fingers pass through him.

But my breath hadn't passed through the lilac petal. No. My breath had intercepted it and diverted it from its course down to the counter. I close my eyes, trying to steal another moment out of the cascades of time.

When I open my eyes, the man and his machine are gone. They'd turned off the lights in the house, and night had fallen. I am alone again.

I take the moment in time to examine the dials and gauges on the Elevan Manus. I see by the gauges that fuses have blown, lines have ruptured. It was overloaded when it sent me forward, and now requires significant repairs before it can halt my progression through time.

I cry out, irrationally and emotionally broken. I can't control myself anymore, can't stop talking to myself and now I'm howling like a rabid dog in the wild. My vocal cords tear and distort the air passing by. In my own ears, my cry is ragged and deafening. Inside the house? Did I even wake them from their sleep? Did they hear me scream? Did they mistake it for a draft in the aging house? A creak of the wood frame? I am here. I still exist. Why shouldn't they hear me?

Before I can perceive the rising of the sun, another day has come. The man is back at his place on the sofa. His device is in his lap now. His filthy stinking bare feet are resting on the

Elevan Manus Machine. The woman is nowhere to be seen.

The sight of this man's feet on my machine obsesses me with disgust. I can't look away. I can't make this moment of time pass as so many other moments have before. I'm locked in. Focused.

My eyes fix on the screen of his machine, that television-typewriter that has captured his soul just as my machine had captured my soul. I strain and direct all my hate towards the device. A crack develops, starting like a pit in a windshield. It crawls outward from the center to the edges of the screen. As the crack grows, it leaves a wake of discoloration on the television screen. The man stands up and spills his coffee. He is quick to pick up his machine off of my machine. The drink beads off the lacquer finish of the Elevan Manus. He evacuates his machine away to the kitchen counter, letting the coffee drip free from it as he goes. He towels it off and swears and inspects the damaged glass. It was too late for his machine. I had killed it. The Elevan Manus, on the other hand, is damaged but ready for repairs and reactivation.

"Come on," I yell at the man. "Throw your broken toy aside and take up my mantle. Invest in the technology before you. Do my work and free me from this cage."

The man keeps his back toward my machine as he goes about trying to repair his own. I reexamine the Elevan Manus, now that it was free of obstructions like the inferior machine and the man's bare feet. The brownish coffee is still pooled on the varnished wood exterior. The sensitive electronics are inside the wooden cask. As long as the fluid stays out, the fragile components inside will be safe. If the fluid leaks into the high voltage equipment inside, it could destroy the entire machine and burn down this house. I kneel down close to the top of the machine. There is a joint where two pieces of wood met. In time-lapsed vision, I see the coffee seep in.

"Towel!" I yelled at the man. What will happen if the machine is destroyed? Will it release me from its influence? Will I be destroyed along with it? I'm not ready to take that risk. "Get a towel and dry this up, immediately. You have no idea what's at stake!"

When I turn towards the kitchen, more time has passed. A new television-typewriter sits recently unboxed on the kitchen table. The man and woman are nowhere to be seen. I turn back to my machine and the pool of coffee is gone, absorbed into the joint.

"No, you damned fools," I say and turn back towards the kitchen.

The man and woman are back again, now dressed for the evening. He is in a suit and she wears a fine black dress.

I walk straight through the man and try to rest my palm on the woman's bare shoulder. I speak into her ear.

"Do something," I say. "Open his eyes to me and to my work. You. You are attuned to me and to the world around you. You drew me to the vase and the lilacs. You know I'm here, don't you?"

Her dress features a bow made of thin fabric sewn to the shoulder strap of her dress. As I speak, the bow, just like the petal, flutters and moves.

"Hear me, woman," I say. "You are my Elizabeth reincarnated. Resurrect my love from its grave. She is gone by now, but you can save me. You can make him carry on my work."

She turns and looks me in the eyes. She smiles and my heart seems to stop.

"Elizabeth, please," I say.

She reaches out her hand. It passes through my body, and connects with the man's hand. She had looked right through me. Her smile belonged not to me, but to the idle idiot who kept me trapped in this hell.

They hold hands and walk out the front door.

Something must be done. I have to put an end to this, regardless of the risks. If this drone of a man can't be inspired to carry on my work, perhaps he can be connived to destroy it. I have no idea if the machine's destruction will free me or lead to my own demise. But I can't stand being in this eternal limbo surrounded by ignorance and sloth. I have a plan, but it must be perfectly executed to work. I have to practice my new ability to interact with the world around me.

I spend seconds of my own time but days of the world's focusing on a few books resting on a shelf. I target just one volume. I strain and concentrate until it hurts to even keep my eyes open. But I remember the essence of the task. Let time spill by until that single finite moment catches my eye, then grasp it in a strangle-hold.

I do just that, and the book tumbles off the shelf.

The woman stands up from her chair next to the sofa, her eyes wide and searching for whoever pulled the book off the shelf, searching for me. She is alone with me in the house.

"Yes," I say as she comes over and sees the book lying sprawled spine-up on the carpet. "Come find me."

She seems to hear a word, or at least a noise. Her head turns, her eyes looking for the source of the sounds like a prey on edge for predators.

"I am here," say to those startled eyes. "And you just might be my redemption."

But time continues to flow over rocks and falls. It takes all my strength to slow down a minute to a speed I can actually experience it. When I weaken, it flows over me as if I'm comatose. Before I could capture that second, she was gone, the book was back on its shelf and the man is back on the sofa with his feet resting on my masterpiece. He ticks and taps on the keys of his device, and I let that moment pass me by. It is a worthless moment.

Night comes. I notice the vase has fresh flowers again. These are tulips. It must be spring time. How many months or even years have ticked by since the lilacs? How many years had drawn their lines across the beautiful face of Elizabeth, and now this woman who is her born-again? I disregard the thought and turn to this new vase and newly-birthed flowers.

I watch the tulips turn from white to egg-shell as they begin to die. I reach out mentally and stop Death's progress as decay creeps across another petal. The inevitable drying, yellowing, and dying cease. I have it. I have this moment.

The vase lifts up off of the counter. My wisps of arms reach out to carry the vase, but it isn't my physical body doing the work. It's my mind's grasp of a moment.

I carried the vase and

the flowers from the kitchen to the living room. The man wasn't there. The woman was gone as well. My actions were going unnoticed, for now. With all the care I can muster, I set the vase down on top of the Elevan Manus Machine.

I'm out of breath, out of energy, out of focus. I am thin. My eyes flutter shut involuntarily as if I'm epileptic. My body, as ghostly as it is, gives in to the all too pedestrian restraint of fatigue. I collapse. Time slips by.

And I'm awake again. Who knows how much time has passed. I come to my feet, although they never really rest on the carpet. Over these moments the couple has perceived as years, I've become

aware of my fictional equivalent. But I'm not just a spirit. I'm not a supernatural specter. I am real and I will shape this world.

I rise, and the couple are here in the living room with me. The couple was coming through the front door, again in fancy evening wear, not the same suit and dress I last saw them in, but

similar. Their faces are similar to when I last saw them, but they've aged. I look into her eyes and for a moment I imagine the years of pain and sorrow Elizabeth had to endure after my disappearance. Is there a chance she is still alive?

I look to my machine and see that despite the years, a vase of flowers remain on top of it. She must have liked where I decided to place them. Lilacs again. Fragrant and violet and beautiful. I turn to the couple. They are embracing. His fingers lace behind her back; hers lace behind his back. After all this time, still no wedding ring. Still no children. Who are these heathens?

They stagger over into the living room, still wrapped up in each other. They near my machine. If they won't discover the secrets inside of Elevan Manus, I'll force them to through pain and violence.

She pushes him back and he lands ass-first on top of my machine. She reaches down and lifts up her dress over her head. Under her dress, she is still as lithe and smooth as ever, as if the years have had no effect. But her beauty is nothing but a distraction to me now, even as she straddles his lap. That they chose the machine on which to consummate their depravity is perfect. If I can't have her or control him, I will destroy them along with the machine.

I must make this one instant matter. Make it true and make myself real.

I focus all my effort on the glass vase. I have managed to slow time to a one second per one second rate, but if I am to truly open their eyes, I have to stop it entirely. He moans. She

writhes. I stop my own blood flowing through my veins. Silence falls as my field of vision narrows on the vase resting next to both of them on top of the Elevan Manus. My vision tunnels black around the lilacs, and in that moment I can reach through it and affect the real world.

The vase shatters. Water splashes out from it, onto his suit and her bare thighs and onto the surface of the machine. Most of the water runs off the side. Some of it pools around the wood

joints. It seeps through. Water falls on bare wire, electrodes and diodes inside, but it's not until the fluid shorts out the massive capacitors that the couple notices.

The man is caught in the electrical current, his palm placed in water. She shoves off of him, saving herself. He convulses. I smile knowing that soon he and the machine will be gone. The woman has found her discarded dress and clutches it against her

chest, a poor attempt to hide her shame. The man froths at the mouth.

I have them both where I want them.

She lunges out and grabs his lapel. She leans backwards and pulls. He breaks contact with the machine and the water and the current. He tumbles to the carpet, out of breath but still alive. It doesn't matter. Destruction of the machine is what matters. The high voltage equipment inside is still smoking and popping.

Can she hear me laugh? Can she sense me next to her?

I watched the short circuit catch the wood on fire. Soon the whole machine will be gone and I will be free from this hell. The machine burns. Time flows on, but at a human's pace. I am attune to it now. I am present.

The woman comes with a fire extinguisher. She hits the handle and releases a cloud of dust and smoke. I am blinded by the white expectorant and so I close my eyes.

When I open them, the fire is out. The man and woman are gone. My machine is also gone. In its place is an inornate coffee table and a fresh vase of tulips. Distrusting my eyes, I approached the table only to reassure myself. My machine had been destroyed, cast aside, and replaced. Still I am here and time carries on at its hurried pace.

The couple comes back through the door, another evening out in formal wear at a formal event. One look at them, one look at her, tells me everything I need to know. Decades have passed. She's white haired and gentle. He is elderly and purposefully firm-footed.

As for me, I hover. I leer around them. My machine is gone but I still remain, no older or younger than I was in 1953. And I understand.

I'll watch this couple live and die, and be replaced by another couple, and a couple after that. My only way to reach out to any of them is through fear and half-heard noises in the night. I move over to this elderly couple, again embracing and standing face to face. My silent footsteps come right behind the woman.

I tell her, "I'm here. I am eternal and alone and terrible. And I will never leave."

A Voice Exhumed

Two work-study students lugged the machine, draped in drop-cloth, into the trailer and sat it on the desk.

"That's fine right there, boys," Professor Darren Johnson said. "Thanks so much."

He waited until they had left the trailer and then slowly approached the hooded mass. Darren grabbed a tail of the oily drop-cloth and yanked.

The machine looked like a steampunk fantasy, levers and gears, knobs and tubes that all seemed too unnecessary and elaborate to be functional. The years and water didn't help. The brass was tarnished almost black. The wood was dried gray like driftwood. Three initials carved into the base, PLM, had almost been erased by years of rot and erosion. He doubted if any of the mechanics worked, whatever they were meant to do.

Darren sat in his chair in his trailer, halfway down the old Arco Mine Pit. They had managed to drain the pit down two hundred feet deep, with another two hundred feet of water until they hit the bottom of the pit and mine tunnels began branching out into narrower veins. There was a basin there at the two hundred foot mark. The original mining community had used the basin for a base camp. Now, Darren and the rest of the crew used it for the same purpose. His was one of several trailers. Some of the work-study kids lived in tents. There were storage containers, floodlight/generator sets, pumps that ran 24/7, and a general noise and bustle about the base camp. But tonight, Professor Johnson was alone in his office trailer, studying the machine, uninterrupted.

Short and pudgy, he wasn't a man respected for his physical aspects. He was a man of mind. Damn what others thought of him for it. His voided wedding ring sat on the desk as well. It served as more of a worry doll these days than an emblem of marriage.

He pushed up his heavy glasses and the sleeves of his soiled button-up shirt. He leaned in closer to the machine that sat on his desk. There was a cracked leather bulb, like the rubber primer on a lawn mower. He pumped it a few times. He threw on an old switch that looked like the kind that set a model train in motion. The machine clanked. Something deep inside the brass and wood case spun softly. One big lever on the side seemed like it should be the last control to be activated. He pulled it down, not without some required effort. It locked into place. The spinning inside the machine stopped.

"Shit," he said, sure he'd broken it.

"Baby? Are you listening?" the machine spoke.

Darren spooked back away from the machine, almost tipping his chair over backward. He was lucky it was on wheels, and rolled back a few feet from his desk and the contraption.

"Can you hear me?" it spoke again. Only it wasn't fair to call it "it." It was a woman. The voice of a woman anyway, soft and maybe just a little scared. "I miss you," she said.

Darren found his heart beating as loud as the generators outside the trailer. His own voice, on the other hand, was dry and muted. What the hell was this machine? A voice recorder he could only guess. But this thing looked more like a chemistry set than the phonograph that was its contemporary. How was it speaking? Where were the sound waves stored? Where did they emit from?

It sighed. No. She sighed, sounding very much human and forlorn. Then she spoke again. "I thought I'd heard you. Guess I was wrong. I should try not to be so hysterical. I love you. Good-bye."

The machine clanked and chortled. Something released the lever on the side and it sprang back up. The whirling deep inside the driftwood case started again, and slowly decrescendoed into silence.

Darren sat pushed away from his desk with his eyes fixated on the old machine. Had it heard him? Was the woman truly waiting for his response? Was it still listening to him now?

"Hell... Hello?" he said.

Only the constant drone of the generators and pumps outside on the basin replied. Then Professor Steve Pennington burst into his trailer. He carried a dozen map sheets and folded newspapers under his wings and a spilling cup of coffee in his hand.

"Darren, I found some of the old records I was looking for. I'd love your take on this stuff. Really compelling stories, man. Check it out," he said and started dropping all the documents on Darren's desk, next to the machine. When he ran out of room, he pushed the machine over to make more space.

"Hey hey hey!" Darren said.

Steve seemed not to hear. "So here's what we already know: The Arco Mine collapsed on August sixth, nineteen twenty-five, burying forty-two souls in rubble and ore. That was well documented in newspapers and oral history. We have names of the forty-two, and they were even able to recover twenty-eight of the forty-two bodies. The mine owner, a Mr. Chester Milford, deemed the vein already mined out and not worth pumping dry again. Milford and his investors picked up and moved to another iron ore vein thirty miles to the east of here. Without Milford and his money and his mining company, the town was left to mourn the tragedy and slowly dried up. The contents and the remaining thirty-four bodies still buried in the mine are forgotten to history."

"Okay," Darren said. "That's all known history."

"Right. But here's what we didn't know. It seems after Milford left town, he didn't want too much bad press about the disaster. Look at this." Steve pulled out a small slip of paper, yellowed, thin and brittle like an onion peel. "This is an invoice from Milford to one of the widows, Miss Ann Crosby for five hundred dollars, a good chunk of money in those days. Here's another one to Miss Darrow, another widow. And another invoice for another five hundred dollars to another widow. He paid out to every one of the forty-two families who lost someone in that mine, except one. There's forty-one invoices and the bank even has a withdrawal on that day for a total of twenty thousand, five hundred dollars."

"So who was the miner who didn't get paid?" Darren asked, his desk now covered in old newspapers, invoices, and ledgers.

"Wasn't a miner," Steve said. "It was his daughter. Phoebe Louise Milford. Her obit says her body was recovered from the mine and buried up by the Milford's home in Duluth. Look at the picture of her here in the paper. She was a beauty, huh? I got a work-study student looking for her tombstone now."

"His daughter? That doesn't make any sense. Why would he let his daughter in an iron mine?"

"A terrific question with a terrific answer," Steve said. "Turns out, she was married to one of Milford's dynamite technicians. A real weirdo from Saint Paul. Charles Joe Fredrichs. Studied at the university and thought of himself as an inventor. He died in the mine too. Do you know what that means?"

Darren shook his head.

"That means, we got a love story in our hands. We got a narrative and with any luck, we'll find some of this Fredrichs guy's tinkerings and we'll have artifacts. You know how much museums pay for this kind of thing? Well, not much, but they pay a hell of a lot more for a love story than they do for old pick axes and carbide lanterns. We might get some real grants for this and with any luck maybe even fund this through its completion! Ha ha!"

Darren's eyes locked on the woman's photo above the obituary. She was pretty. Her face was smoothed by youth and the soft focus of the photograph. Her hair was short and in tight curls, like one of those Art Deco women from a Fitzgerald novel. She wore pearls. She was looking off camera. Something about her eyes told Darren that she wasn't really seeing anything, like what she was looking for was a million miles away. Or more likely, 200 feet underground.

"But how did she die? Why would she be in the mine?"

"You got me," Steve said. "But you know what I think? I don't think she was in the mine. I think she was right here." Steve pointed at the floor.

Darren couldn't respond. He was confused.

"Think about it. We're using this basin as a base camp. Why wouldn't they? I bet she had a nice little cottage right here, well below the high water mark, so she could be that much closer to her lover boy. When they set that fateful charge of dynamite below Lake Huntington the mine flooded out in less than fifteen minutes. My guess it that she was sleeping right up to the point her little cottage filled with lake water."

"That's terrible," Darren said.

"No. That's a tragic love story that's going to keep us rolling in grant money," Steve said. The machine next to and under all of his papers finally caught his eye. "What's this?"

"It's... Actually, I have no idea."

"Does it work? What the hell is it supposed to be?"

"I honestly don't know. Hey, be careful with it."

"Look. PLM. Phoebe... What was her middle name? Yep! Phoebe Louise Milford," Steve said, articulating the words as he pointed to the initials carved into the machine's wood base. "Oh man! This is great. I'm willing to bet my right nut that old Fredrichs built this for her. You gotta figure out what this thing was supposed to do."

"Okay. Okay. I'm working on it. Just..." Darren was flustered. "I need some time."

"Do you need help? I got an engineering major who is just sorting chunks of iron ore and petrified stool samples into piles. He might be able to- Hold on." Steve pulled a buzzing cell phone from his pocket. "This is the girl I sent to Duluth looking for that tombstone. Hello? Yeah. Did you find it?"

Darren watched his colleague walk out of the trailer as eager and as distracted as a freshmen student. With a screech and a bam of the screen door, Steve was swallowed by the constant drone of generators and pumps. Darren turned back to his desk.

The machine was half buried in the papers Steve had abandoned. He'd probably be gone for hours, distracted by the next odd bit of newspaper that caught his attention. Steve was a child, but he was also right. If they didn't find a way to tell the story of the mining disaster in a way that grabbed people's attention, money would dry up and Arco Mine would be abandoned a second time.

But the machine. It spoke to him. Not just spoke like a phonograph. But spoke to him like it was a telephone. Only it had no wires, ear or mouth piece. Charles Friedrichs could have given his wife a phone and strung wire down into the depths of the mine, but instead he built her this thing. It functioned more like a radio, but there was nothing that resembled a diode or antenna that would be capable of transmitting through two hundred feet of rock and iron. What Darren was imagining was impossible.

Darren checked over his shoulder to the door. No sign of Steve and his babblings. He turned back to the machine. How did he work it before? What had Steve messed up by monkeying with it? Darren cleared away the papers.

The paper had rubbed away some of the tarnish. The brass underneath seemed eager to return to a shine. Darren went to work the controls. The bulb. The switch. The whirling started back up. Darren pulled the lever. The machine went silent.

"Hello?" he said and immediately felt stupid. Still, he got up from his chair, went to the trailer door and slid the locking chain into the groove. At the sound of the chain sliding against metal, all the hairs stood up on his arms. He was certain the machine had made a noise precisely when the chain rattled.

He turned around, the span of the trailer seeming awfully distant. The machine sat amongst the old invoices and obits like a hibernating grizzly.

"Hello?" Darren called to it.

"I hear you," Phoebe said back. He knew it was her, could pin her fragile voice to the face in the black and white newspaper picture. It wasn't a machine. She was a ghost caught in time. "Is that you baby? You sound so far away."

He was sweating. More than usual. What the hell was he supposed to say? What could he possibly have to say to a dead woman?

"Yes. Yes, it's me," he lied. "I'm here."

"Oh. Well, that's good. How are things down there? Are you finding lots of gold and silver, or just that cruddy old iron?"

Darren laughed. He crept across the trailer, closer to the machine and the voice. "No silver or gold. Lots of iron ore though."

"Well, I suppose that will make daddy happy," Phoebe said. "And how about you, my love? Are you happy down there, in the dark?"

Darren was back to his chair now, just a few feet from his desk. "I'm, uh... I'm okay. It's dark." This wasn't a lie. It was dark outside and not much brighter inside the trailer. "But it's good to hear your voice." Also not a lie. She terrified him, but also fascinated him. And her voice had a soothing quality to it. Darren understood immediately the motivation to build this contraption.

"Come back up," she said. "I want you here with me."

"I- I don't think I can do that, dear," he said.

Then next time she spoke, some of the innocence was gone from her tone. "You sound different than when we spoke yesterday, but you say the same things. You don't need to be down there. We don't need the money. I've told you, we'll have more money than we'll ever need. You say that you love me and miss me, but if that's so, why don't you come back up to me?"

Darren smiled. "If only I could. If only I could come to you and look you in the eyes." He wheeled his chair up to the machine and lifted the picture of this woman off his desk.

"Tomorrow?" she asked him.

That voice... How could he tell her no? "What, ah... What is the date tomorrow?"

"You've been down there too long, I think you'll turn into a mole soon. Tomorrow is Thursday, the sixth."

"August sixth," Darren said. His eyes locked on the dates listed on the obituary.

Born May 19th, 1906. Died August 6th, 1925.

"Charles? My love? What's the matter?" she said to him.

"I... I have to go. I can't talk," Darren said. He fumbled with the machine's controls. He tugged on the large lever but it wouldn't budge. He tried the lever but it flipped with no effect.

Phoebe kept talking. "Charlie. Is something wrong?"

"I... I'm sorry," Darren said. He found another switch and tried that. The big lever on the side released and sprung up into its original position. The machine transmitted no static or noise aside from the woman's voice, but somehow Darren knew as soon as the lever returned to its upward position, the call was over. The soft spinning inside the case was back, but only for a short time. Within seconds it ran down and everything was quiet, except the diesel engine droning coming from outside the trailer.

What the hell was he doing?

The machine haunted him through the rest of the night. He struggled to keep it out of his vision and ignore its existence. He buried it in the newspapers, much like the woman in Duluth and the man she was still trying to reach two hundred feet down in the mine. He tried to sleep on the old couch in the trailer, but sleep wouldn't come. When he closed his eyes he saw her face. When the engines outside the trailer harmonized into a white noise, he could hear her voice. He came close to sleep. His conscious thought grew more confused and fatigued. When the machine clanked and clamored back to life, he was sure it was a dream.

"Baby? I know you're down there. Why won't you speak?"

Darren sat up. He was just wearing old gym shorts, his round belly hanging over the waistband. He felt embarrassed and intimidated by the voice. She was a classic beauty, and he was a modern slob. Still, she wouldn't be ignored.

"I miss you," she said. "I'm lonely. No one here will even acknowledge I exist. They're all afraid of daddy. But not you. So talk to me."

The silence broke him. "Okay. Okay, I'll talk. I just don't know what to say to you."

"Well that's a silly thing to say. Just hearing your voice is enough," she said.

"But I don't understand what will happen. I don't know the rules. The cause and effect. I don't think I should interfere with what's going to happen to you. I don't know if I should or if I even can change what happens."

"What are you talking about? Nothing is going to happen to me. Baby, you're talking nonsense," she said from inside the driftwood case. "Just... tell me about your day. How about that?"

"I was talking with a colleague," Darren said. "We were talking about your family's place in Duluth. Is it nice there?"

"Charles, you've been there."

"I know. I know." The lies were coming easier now. They felt invited by her, demanded even. "But how do you like it? Would you be happy there?"

"You know I like it there. The view of Lake Superior is spectacular. I could watch the ships pass under the lift-bridge and come in and out of port all day. It's cold and windy and wet, I know. But I don't care. There's something I love about how sullen it is when the chill comes off the lake," Phoebe said. "But we can live anywhere you want to take me."

"Do you like these machines?" Darren asked.

"They're amazing," she said. "When we're all finished up here you must take them to the patent office in Saint Paul. You'll be famous, for certain."

"Could you do me a favor?" Darren said.

"Maybe," she said, more mischievous than Darren anticipated. "Do you want me to tell you what I dream about when I dream of us together?"

"No. No, no. I just need something simple," Darren said.

"Oh. Well. Okay."

"Do you have something sharp? Something that will dig into wood?"

"Well, I guess the needle on my brooch is sharp. What in heavens do you want me to do?"

Darren paused and readied himself for what might come. "I want you to take your brooch and scrape some marks into the front of the machine. Maybe just to the right of your initials."

"Scrape it? But honey, the finish is brand new. It's so beautiful."

"Just... I'm sure it is beautiful. But I need you to do this. To make the machine work properly."

She paused. He leaned in close, his face just a foot away from the wooden base of the machine. "Well, I never understood how any of this works. So if you insist," Phoebe said. Darren waited.

Slowly, awkwardly, small groves appeared next to the more elegantly carved PLM. When they first appeared, the freshly exposed wood looked young and fresh. An instant later, a near century of dry rot caught up and the wood turned from honey yellow to bone gray.

"Okay. I did it. Can you hear me any better now?"

"A little better, yeah," Darren said. There was no change to her voice, aside from sounding just slightly more innocent and vulnerable. But it helped Darren make up his mind. "Okay, my dear. I need you to do one more thing."

"Anything," she said.

"Go to Duluth. Leave tonight; tomorrow will be too late. Pack a few things and wait for me there where you watch the ships come in. I know the place. I'll meet you there in just a while. Can you do that for me?"

"Tell me you love me," she said.

"What?"

"Say that you love me," she said. "You haven't told me lately, and you haven't acted like it lately, spending all your time down there in the mines, and now this? Say it. Say that you love me."

"I... Phoebe... It's just..." Darren's shoulders slouched. "I love you."

"I love you more," she said. "Now, no more talk of me leaving you for Duluth. You and I are in this together."

"I... I guess. What time is it there? Up there I mean?"

"Same time as down there, my love. It's late. Will you stay with me until I fall asleep? I miss hearing you breathe as I drift off."

"That sounds wonderful," Darren admitted. There was something too soothing about her voice. It penetrated the reality of the situation. He was vaguely aware of the rarity and tragedy of spending his night with this woman on the last night she'd be alive. "What if I fall asleep before you?"

"That's okay. I'm sure your day was long and full of toil. Go ahead and fall asleep. I'll be here for you in the morning."

Darren rested his head on his desk amongst the obituaries, articles, the machine, and the sound of her relaxed breathing. He wheezed but was sure that something about the machine translated his apneatic breathes into something reassuring on the far side. Hers were like a melody. It wasn't long before he was asleep.

He woke up with a start, confused again between dream and reality. When he lifted his head up, he squinted at the pre-dawn glow seeping through the blinds in his trailer. He'd slept through the night. Today was the day of the flood, the day the woman died. He panicked.

"Miss Milford? Phoebe? My darling, are you there?" he asked.

The machine was dead. It sat there as still as a 90 year old artifact should. He cleared the papers away from its base and saw the PLM and the fresh but ancient scrapes next to those letters. There was still time. He could impact the past. He could save her. Maybe save all of them.

"Phoebe! My love! Talk to me!" he called into the machine.

The large lever was back in the up position. The machine had ran dry during the night. He just needed to prime it and reset the controls. The leather bulb. He primed it with squeezes from his sweaty hand. Shouldn't it be whirling by now? No. First, the switch. He triggered it.

The machine whirled. Whatever internal mechanisms inside of it still functioned. He waited while it slowed and softened. The whirl never stopped. It just sunk below the audible threshold. He held his breath, listening for any hint of it. There was none. Hopefully she'd still be there. Hopefully she'd still be alive in her time. Last was the lever.

"Phoebe? Are you there?" he said.

"My love? Is that you?"

She was there. "I need to know something. What time is it there?" He rifled through the various articles and newspapers Steve had left there until he found the information he was looking. His wedding band, now signifying nothing but broken promises, rolled to the floor. He ignored it. His eyes fixed on the piece of data he needed. 7:15 AM. That was when the flood began, immediately after the first blast of the day. Darren checked his own watch. 6:25. He had time.

"Don't worry," she said. "I didn't forget to wind my watch. It's a quarter after seven in the morning."

"No. No it should be just before six thirty. Why..." Daylight savings time. It hadn't been enforced in her time, only in his time. The flood had already begun.

"Baby. What's the matter?"

Would it really matter if he told her? Could he really affect the past? If he did, what would become of her? The machine? The dig? What if he just let her believe that he was her beloved, all the way up until her death? It wouldn't be long now. Another five minutes and the mine flood would fill the entire mine, her cottage included. Five minutes wasn't that much time to keep up a lie.

"Phoebe. Say that you love me," he spoke into the machine.

"You know I do, my darling. I love you until the end of time."

"Listen to me very carefully," Darren said. He breathed in deep. "I'm not who you think I am. I'm not your husband."

"What? What are you talking about?" her soft voice found an edge. "Who are you then? Where did you come from?"

"Listen. There was an accident this morning in the mine. At seven fifteen, the miners blew into Lake Huntington. The mine will flood to the very top by seven thirty. That's five minutes from now. You can escape, but you have to go now. Go! Go to Duluth and never think of this place again."

"Who are you? Why are you saying such things? Why have you *lied* to me?"

"I- I can't explain. I'm sorry. You sounded so beautiful. I didn't think you were real." Darren scrambled to try to make her understand. But none of that mattered now. "I'm a professor from the future, an archeologist studying the site of your death. This machine spoke to me. You spoke to me. I see the marks you made in the machine. You can get out. I can save you!"

"Where is my husband? What happened to my husband?"

"He's... He's still down there. Even to this day," Darren said. Strange how when he committed to truth, it came so easy. "His body was never recovered from the disaster."

"Are you telling me he's...? Oh god," she trailed off. Darren heard echoes of her voice coming from far away from her machine.

Darren closed his eyes. It wasn't hard to imagine her stepping outside of her cottage on the basin and looking down into the abyss below, quickly filling with cold lake water. He heard her scream his name. "Charles! Charlie! God damn, you, no!"

Darren imagined there was debris, flotsam and jettison rising up with the flood waters from its underground source. Likely bodies too. Phoebe was there, standing on the edge of the basin, watching death swallow everything in her life and racing to swallow her too.

"Climb," Darren muttered, knowing she couldn't hear. "Just climb."

There were noises coming from the other side of the machine. The bang of a door. Footsteps. Panting. Then her voice, sounding more jagged and hateful than he ever imagined it could be.

"I don't know who you are, sir. I'm going down there with my husband. I wish I could take you with us. This deep, it's sure to be a short trip to hell," she said. "When I come back, I'll be sure to retrieve your deceitful pathetic soul."

And that was it. The machine clunked and the big lever sprang back into its upward position. Something inside spun for a few seconds and then it was dead.

"No," Darren moaned. "Phoebe? Don't do it. Come back and live."

He tried the machine. The bulb. The switch. It spun and seemed ready for transmission. The lever. He called. She didn't respond. She was gone.

It wasn't too much longer when Darren's cell phone rang. He sat up to find himself leaning into his desk, crying into his arms, wetting the records Steve had brought him, like an overgrown man-child. He took two rings to compose himself before picking up the phone to see who was calling.

It was Steve. Darren tried to clear his thoughts, readying himself to sound professional.

He didn't get a chance to say hello. Steve started right in. "Darren! You won't believe it, man. After my work-study called I had to come out here and see it for myself. Sorry about leaving you like that. I really wanted to take a closer look at that artifact you found. But listen, I got to ask you something, and be honest."

"Okay," Darren said.

"Did you tell anybody, and I mean *anybody* about Phoebe Louis Milford? Particularly about her grave up here in Duluth?"

"What? No. Who would I tell?"

"I don't know. Doesn't matter. Here's the deal: Someone exhumed her," Steve said.

"What? What do you mean?"

"Yeah, bud. Somebody dug her up. I mean, we haven't dug down to look in the casket yet, but the gravesite has definitely been tampered with. I mean, from all indications, someone dug up her bones or at least dug down to the casket itself. We're waiting for a court order before we can dig further but, wow! How wild is this, huh? I mean, whether we find her bones down here or not, I'm sure we're going to come across some really interesting stuff, from an archaeological standpoint. You need to get here, man. Once we get that court order, well, we're not waiting for you. Get your ass to Duluth!"

With that, Steve hung up and left him in silence yet again.

"But... I... I need to get dressed," Darren told himself.

Before he could get up, he heard her voice again. His eyes locked on the machine.

"Baby, can you hear me? Are you listening?" she said.

Darren froze in place. His heart thumped louder than the generators and pumps outside. "Yes. I hear you. Are you alive?"

She spoke again, and this time Darren realized her voice was much more rich and stereophonic than before. "I came back for you." It was like she was right behind him.

Darren turned and saw Phoebe Louis Milford standing there in his filthy, cramped trailer. She was slim and draped in a satin white dress stretching from her small chest to her ankles. Her pearls were soiled and broken, dangling around her neck. Her tightly wound hair was rotting and falling out. Her once porcelain-smooth skin was now papyrus over bone. Her exposed teeth were half missing and yellowed like an old stain. She stretched out one hand, as if he'd take it and let her lead him.

"I came back for you, since you wanted to be so close. I'm here to bring you underneath with the rest of us."

He stretched his hand out to hers.

Thin Lions

I stuck the gun sights in front of my aiming eye. The doughy security guard stood beyond the barrel, shaking in his shoes, completely unprepared for the idea that his fifteen dollar an hour job might one day put a bullet into his head.

"Sorry pal. It's just business," I said to him.

I pulled the trigger and he crumpled. A chorus of screams sang all around me, each one cut short in fear that their scream might be the longest, the most attention-drawing, the most annoying to the gunman. This little Indian casino on this tiny rez was full of frail old white people just looking to burn through their social security check. They never asked for this, but I'd give it to them anyway. I ignored the crowd and turned the barrel to the gal at the till inside her little booth. The door to the booth was already open, thanks to the sorry sack leaking blood and brain matter onto the casino carpet.

"Why? Why why why why…" she rambled.

It sounded rhetorical and since she was already loading straps of cash into duffel bags for me, I probably didn't need to answer. I did anyway.

"Why? Because some people are born with a piece of the pie crammed in their mouths. This is me, cutting my own slice," I told her.

When she had three duffel bags full, I decided that was enough. I slung one over each shoulder and held the third in my left hand. I kept the .45 in my right hand and panned it across the crowd of gamblers and geriatrics. Just to keep them from spawning any bright ideas, I dumped six rounds into the ceiling.

"If you didn't have any stories to tell your grandkids, you do now," I told them. "You're welcome."

I backed out through the fire exit. When I went through the door, the alarm sounded like a slot machine paying out. Jackpot, baby.

There were no security cameras on the back side of the casino. Just some dumpsters and employee parking. Kim was waiting for me there in the pickup with the lights off. I dumped the three duffel bags in the rusted-out bed and hopped in the cab. She met me with a sloppy, whiskey-flavored kiss. "God damn, you are sexy," she told me.

"You think I didn't know that? Hit the gas, bitch," I said.

She did, and we were gone.

#

They say crime don't pay. I say it pays too well. What the hell was I going to do with all that cash? We spent the next two days blowing money and jumping towns. The duffel bags never seemed to get any lighter. How was I supposed to know a little podunk Indian casino in the middle of nowhere would have so much ching on hand?

I sat in the cheap desk chair in the even cheaper motel room we'd rented somewhere north of Brainerd. I was dressed to the nines. Tailored suit. Double woven silk tie. Rayban sunglasses. Shoes polished to look like funhouse mirrors. The .45 sat in my lap, still loaded for bear.

Kim was jumping on the bed in just her undies and my Motörhead t-shirt, throwing the hundreds around like confetti. She was whooping and singing along with Katy Perry. She only stopped to spill whiskey down her mouth and all over my t-shirt. Sounds like the perfect woman, but you don't know Kim.

She choked down another gulp of Crown Royal. "Get over here you dapper son of a bitch and give me some of that high class love. This shit ain't no trailer park pussy anymore."

Her eyes were lit up. My shirt draped off her shoulder and exposed her silk smooth skin below her collarbone. Her nipples were poking through the thin black fabric of my shirt, just below the text, "Born to Lose." The way she held that bottle, her fingers fumbling but delicate. Okay. I admit it. She looked good enough to eat. Maybe I'd show her a good time on that bed with the cash all around us like in that one Demi Moore movie. There was enough of it.

That's not why I robbed the place. I don't know if I can explain why I did it. All I can say is that if you were in my shoes inside that casino, if you felt the power running out from my heart through the barrel of that .45 … I wouldn't need to explain it.

As far as pulling it off, we got lucky. There was no Ocean's 11-style plot. There was no plan beyond, "Pull the truck around back and keep the motor running." There happened to be one overweight security guard and zero cops anywhere near the casino. No one saw us coming, and no one saw us go. We were two states away and almost two million dollars richer. One point eight million dollars roughly. That's not even counting what we'd already burnt through. Clothes. Booze. Some guy had a Dodge Charger parked on the street corner for sale. I bought it all in twenties, gave him a bogus name for the title and drove off without making a dent in our haul.

So there you go kiddos. Crime pays. At least it paid me.

She peeled off my thousand dollar suit. I pulled off her underwear and lifted up the Motörhead shirt. We got filthy with each other. The money stuck to our sweaty skin. The .45 bounced on the mattress with the safety off.

Kim loved all this. She was a millionaire in that moment. Nevermind we were living in a motel overrun by mites and bedbugs and other people's dried up filth. Nevermind what we were going to do with all this cash tomorrow, or the next day, or the day after that. She loved the idea of being a millionaire, but had no idea what that really meant.

What was I supposed to do, take this cash and invest it in a CD? An IRA? Should I go Roth or traditional? Put it in a mutual fund? Buy a house? Settle down?

Get respectable? Get married and have kids? Man, if I wanted to do that, I wouldn't be out robbing casinos to begin with.

We laid on the bed, catching our breath. She turned to me and whispered, "We did it, babe. We made it. We're set for fucking life."

"Get off the money," I told her.

"Why? Where are we going?" she asked.

"I'm going to burn it. All of it," I said.

"But... Why?"

"Cause fat lions don't hunt."

#

We drove out to an abandoned camp site. I popped the trunk of the Charger and pulled out the three duffel bags and a plastic can of gasoline. Kim got out of the car but just stood next to the passenger door. She managed to put on a pair of daisy dukes when we left the hotel, but she was still wearing my t-shirt.

"You're just fucking with me. I know it," she said, not believing her own words. "You don't have the stones to burn that money."

She watched me dump the cash in the fire pit and douse the pile in gas. I waited for her to realize I wasn't bluffing.

"You light that match and we go right back to where we started. A pair of losers. Nothing but two jobless white trash chumps slumming at a fucking campsite," she said.

"Take a good look, sweetheart," I said. "You might not recognize the champ left standing when this money's gone."

I flicked open a Zippo and held the flame up between me and her so she could see it. Then I tossed it over my shoulder. The flames lit up the woods and cast my long shadow out in front of me. A wave of heat enveloped my back. I walked away. She screamed. We passed each other, me strolling back to the Charger, her charging to the burning cash.

I got to the driver's door and turned around. The flames must have been fifteen goddamn feet tall. I thought the whole forest was going to burn down around us. Kim was on her knees in front of the fire pit, reaching into the flames, pulling out stacks of twenties or hundreds with each fist. She was still screaming. Crying now. Her skin was boiling off her arms. Her pretty blonde hair caught flame. She thought the money was permanent. She wanted to save it. She never counted on getting more money down the road in the next town. For her, this was a fucking 401K.

I came back to our little camp fire with the .45. She didn't even notice me put the barrel to her head. I shot her through the back of the skull and kicked her onto the heap. She loved the money so much, she could go straight to hell with it.

What a shame. I loved that t-shirt.

#

I pulled up to the next heist in the Charger, still decked out like an American Outlaw James Bond. I left the car running and the Ray Bans on as I walked into the bank.

Forget casinos. Sure, they paid out well enough, too well really, but they were low class. It didn't feel right stealing from poor people anyway. No. It was going to be banks for me from that day forward.

It was broad daylight out. I didn't bother with a mask or gloves. I wanted the cameras to see my face. Let the evening news tell the whole country about me.

I pushed open the glass doors and went straight for the counter. I cut the line to the teller.

Someone got offended and said, "Hey, buddy!"

I pulled out the .45 and fired a shot into the ceiling. Plaster and asbestos fluttered down around me like snow. The next second everyone was lying on the floor and the women behind the counter were filling sacks with cash. I didn't even have to say a word.

About then, I noticed the teller on the left. She looked through my polarized lens. Blonde hair. Fire-lit eyes. I looked at her and saw no fear, but hunger instead. I went up to her.

"Ever been with a self-made millionaire?" I asked her. She shook her head no. Of course she hadn't. That's why she was running a till at the local branch.

"Do you want to?" I said.

She didn't smile, but blushed in a way that told me she did.

"Come on, babe. Let's go for a ride."

Vomit Monsters

Oh God, here it comes again.

The creature stretches my esophagus wide. Its stiletto legs jab and claw its way up. I gag. Cough. It feels like throwing up broken glass or a wad of barbed wire the size of a softball. My neck bulges out. By the time those 16D-nail legs reach my throat and start to pull its thorax into my mouth I'm relieved. The worst part, its trip up its backward birth canal, is almost over.

I open wide. The thing's pointed legs reach out past my lips like a drowning man reaching out of a lake. The legs grip flesh and I feel it pull itself loose. It falls out of my mouth, as eager to exit me as I am to have it out. The vomit monster tumbles to the snow and slush mixture that covers the alley behind Gene's Irish Pub and drags a string of saliva and bile out of my mouth along with it.

I'm on all fours, half drunk, my knees wet and my hands numb from the cold. Back in the bar, when I felt the thing start to crawl up from my guts I dedicated myself to one sole purpose: get away from anyone who might see and get rid of the beast.

It writhes in the snow and slush and drool only for a few seconds. Just enough time to sort out up from down. Then like a newly birthed zebra, it puts its pointed lobster-like legs against the concrete and starts to scramble out of the alley. It's small, despite how big it felt coming up, about the shape and size of a Coke bottle. Its mouth is as wide as the bottom of a bottle, and its tail turned to a nub about as wide as a cap. It's pale and hairless and wrinkled like those cats that looks like demons. Its pink skin suggest it's some kind of mammal. Its legs say crustacean. Its sphincter-like mouth with its rings of teeth say it's part lamprey. I say one hundred percent abomination.

It scrambles and squirms to the entrance of the alley.

No one can ever know about this.

I put one boot underneath me and then the other. I stagger on two uncertain feet, but just for a moment. No time to dawdle. I pulled the 1911 .45 caliber ACP from the inside of my soiled Carhartt coat and level the tritium sites at the squirming retreating vomit monster. I thumb off the safety and pull the trigger.

The thing explodes just two feet from the street side. The echoes off the walls of the alley make my ears ring like I just left a Mötley Crüe concert.

I put the safety back on and pocket the gun. The stomach acid dangles off my sleeve after I wipe it off my chin. I kick the remains of the creature aside and head back to the bar. There is not much left of it. As I reach the sidewalk and street front it's clear no one heard the gunshot.

Gene's Irish Pub is warm and loud. The place smells like people, beer, and the free popcorn out of the machine in the back. It's Friday night. The place is packed. Bob Seger is on the radio. As I moved through the crowd, I burp and self-consciously wipe my mouth for left-over drool. I weave past the last few patrons between me and the bar and my stool comes into view. I wasn't gone long, but I see three shot glasses lined up in front of my empty stool. Hank and Tommy are on either side. Hank spots me first.

"Hey, Aaron! We got a little surprise for ya," he calls to me.

"Three wisemen," Tommy says. "We did ours now you gotta do yours."

They pat my back and rough me up as I sit down, all in fun of course. I look at the three shots all lines up like civil war soldiers ready to die in battle. Jim Bean, Jack Daniels and Jose Cuervo. The three wisemen. Yea.

That's when Barb comes up on the other side of the bar. Barb. She had to be smoking hot back in her day. These days her face was wrinkled, eyes a bit baggy, tits a bit saggy. Still, she looks damn good for her age. After the three shots she'll look even better.

I'm no spring chicken either.

I can't help but think the things inside of me are there because of something I did or something I am. Ain't no young studs puking up barf babies in the back alley. Should've taken better care of myself. Should have come from better stock. Shouldn't be such a slug.

"Come on, big boy," Barb says. "They ain't gonna drink themselves."

I smile at her and take up the first soldier in formation. Jim. Down the hatch. The shot glass makes a heavy knock against the wood bar when I set it down. Now Jack's turn. I shoot it. The whiskey burns especially hot where the creature had scraped with its legs. I hold the Jack down and knock that empty glass against the wood. One more. Jose. God, I hate tequila. Oh well. I take up the last standing soldier and dump him down my throat, right past the tongue and straight down the hatch.

"Ish, that tastes good," I manage to say as I set the last glass down on the bar.

"Damn, Aaron, you're pretty good at sucking guys down," she says to me. "Not as good as me, but you're getting there."

She winks as she picks up the glasses and wipes away with a rag what I spilled. I admit it. I love trashy women.

Hank whoops. Tommy shoves my shoulder. They swear and laugh. They're good drinking buddies; almost good enough for me to forget what's been coming from inside of me. My head spins. Another three drinks like that and I just might forget.

Hank slides a can of beer into my hand. I wash out the residual burn of whiskey and tequila. My throat is soothed by the cold beer. Good for the mind. Good for the body. I put elbows on the bar and cross my right arm under my left. My right hand rests inside my coat and my fingers run along the terrain of the .45. It's comforting, knowing whatever comes out of me I can put down with a fifty cent bullet. As long as I have the gun I know I'm okay.

I usually don't carry when I drink. It's not responsible. I didn't used to carry at all. It was unnecessary. Now? With these things coming up out of me every other day or so? I always carry.

Hank and Tommy joke and laugh and bitch about our shitty football team is playing this year. I ignore them. My hand tucked inside my coat probes my stomach, feeling for more of these Coke-bottle sized parasites. How many have come out of me now? When will I run out of these things? How were they getting inside of me? Some really bad food I ate maybe. Had to be. I guess they had to start out small and grow inside of me like a some giant mutated tapeworm.

First time I puked one I was on the job, installing traffic signs for the city. We were in on the edge of town where things always get a little weird. Just our work truck and oak trees stripped of their leaves. Bitter cold out that day. Nowhere to hide. I had to go to the other side of the work truck to hawk up the bald lobster-weasel stomach-slug. Lucky enough, we were done installing the sign by the time I had the thing up and out of me. I stared at the thing like it was an alien dropped off from Mars as it twisted and curled on the ice and pavement. Eventually, Hank yelled for me to get my ass in the truck. I'm sure the creature frozen to death out there in the cold. For Christ's sake, I hope it froze to death.

The second one killed my dog. Well, it would have if I hadn't put a bullet through it and through poor old Max's head all in one shot. I buried both of them in my backyard. Couldn't bring him into the vet, not with that thing latched onto him. Even after I put a bullet through it, the creature's mouth was clamped tight to the base of my dog's neck, just below the collar. Couldn't pry it loose. Not even with a screwdriver.

It's a damn shame. I loved that dog more than any human I know.

The third one I was ready for. Had the .45 loaded and ready on my nightstand. Woke up right out of a dead sleep as soon as it started to crawl up my throat. Even made it to the toilet. Had to buy a new toilet after I made my deposit in the bowl and went about blasting it to shards. Killed the creature though.

Number four is a splatter in the alley out back.

And they were becoming more frequent. Shit. I haven't even installed the new toilet yet.

I take a long pull off the beer. Beer will help me forget. Besides, there can't be too many more left in me. If I had any say over it, I'd go out back and puke the rest out right now. Just so long as no one found me. No one can know about this. They'll quarantine me. Operate on me. Do news reports. Might as well put me in a circus sideshow. "Come see the Monster Pukin' Man!" No thanks. I can handle this without any special attention.

"Hey," I nudge Hank. "Did I tell you my dog died the other day?"

"Whadja say?"

The music is loud. I lean over and yell in his ear, "My dog died. Max. He died."

"Oh shit. I'm sorry, man. That sucks," he says back. He lifts up his beer. "To your dog."

I lift up my beer.

Hank yells to Tommy, "Hey, you too!"

"What?"

"We're drinking to Aaron's dog!" he yells.

"His dog?"

"Yeah. His fucking dog died the other day. Raise your drink!" Hank yells.

Then Barb comes back over. "Hey, whoa. What are you guys drinking to?"

"Aaron's dog," Hank yells and slurs. "Little fucker keeled over."

"Your dog died?" she asked.

I nod.

"Well, I'm drinking too then," she says and pours herself a shot. "To… What was your dog's name?"

"Max!" Hank yells.

"To Max!" Barb says and we all bring our drinks together. Cans don't really clink the way a good toast should. Still, I drink. To Max.

I watch Barb walk away with her empty glasses. Her ass is a better distraction than the beer. Big and round and just the right amount of bounce. Not bad. Not bad at all. I could be satisfied here in this moment with Barb and the guys. With a good buzz and my free hand touching the pistol grip of the .45. With my barf babies blown apart in the alley or frozen solid along the side of some dark and empty road on the way out of Dead Oaks. I could watch that ass all night.

So of course, I start to feel another one tickle the bottom of my throat. I don't know how deep down my esophagus my nerves start, but that's where I feel the creature, at the very bottom. Fuck! Another one? How? How many are in there?

Maybe I'm being paranoid. Maybe it's just the alcohol. Tequila never set well with my stomach. Maybe I can just throw up some gas station hot dogs and chicken wings instead of a hell-spawned mutant tapeworm. Maybe if I'd eaten the bones with the chicken wings. I have no idea what the things are crawling up out of me, but they're sharp.

I start to hurk. If I don't leave now, I'm going to birth this one right here on the bar. Right in front of Hank, Tommy, Barb and all the other lowlifes blowing their Friday's paychecks before Saturday's sunrise. With this crowd there was no way I was going to make it back out to the alley. Not again. I'm trapped. Stuck here surrounded by a hundred assholes with a monster crawling up my guts.

Barb. I watch her move her ass pass the three of us and head to the women's room. Good idea. Fantastic idea! The men's room is right next to the women's. No way I can make it outside to the alley, but if I can make it to a bathroom stall…

"Gotta go," I manage to say to Hank and Tommy. I shove away from the bar and start forcing myself through the crowd.

Oh God. This one is coming quick. I try to hold it down, as if I can squeeze my throat tight enough to force it back down. It's no use. This one is aggressive, climbing up my throat like a monkey on a ladder. A bald little monkey with knives for hands and the Sarlacc Pit for a mouth. I shove the last drunk between me and the men's room out of the way. I dare not talk or the little bastard at the back of my mouth will come shooting out of me. The guy bitches, but I push open the bathroom door and duck inside faster than he can protest.

The thing is almost up. I feel its spiky legs dig into my tongue and the roof of my mouth.

It's a small bathroom. One sink. One pisser. One toilet stall. And what do you know, there's one son of a bitch in the stall. I hear it flush and have hope. I pull on the stall door just as the guy inside turns the latch. I almost rip the flimsy door off the hinges.

"Jesus, man," he says.

I want to scream at him to get the hell out of my way. What I'm able to get out is an onomatopoeia that sounds something like, "Hhhhhnnnnnnnnggggh!" The stiletto spikes of the creature are protruding through my clenched teeth like the fangs of the Predator from that Arnold movie. I don't have time to remember what it was called. I'm puking a fucking demon up here.

The guy recoils from me and dips out of the bathroom as fast as he can. I slam the shitter stall door behind me but don't have time to latch it, so it just bounces back open. Fuck it. I collapse in front of the Porcelain God and loosen my clamped jaw. The creature jumps right out.

It misses the toilet and lands somewhere behind the bowl, knocking over the plunger sitting on a piss stained paper plate. The creature's hard-tipped legs click and clack against the syrup-sticky tile floor. It slips behind the bowl before I can get the 1911 out of my coat. I push myself away from toilet with my boots and point the gun.

This one is quick. It scrambles out under the stall wall before I can fire a shot. I fire a shot anyway. Shards of tile spray out from the bullet hole in the floor. The stall door swung back shut, so I shove it open again and come out of the stall on my feet, the barrel of my .45 scanning for the vomit monster. It's quick. Under the pisser. Under the sink. I can't get a shot.

Just then some numbnut opens the bathroom door and out it goes. This moron, he doesn't even know. He just came in here to tap his keg and found some maniac swinging around a hand cannon like he's got something against men's rooms. He swears and realizes whatever I got going on in here is more important than the pressure in his bladder. He leaves the men's room, and I'm right on his heels.

As soon as I'm back into the bar I bury the .45 inside my jacket but keep my eyes focused on the floor for the creature. I see shoes, work boots, crushed popcorn kernels, old gum... There! Just as I spot the bastard it slips into the gap under the door of the women's bathroom. Momma raised a gentlemen, but there's a time to be a gentlemen and there's a time to shoot vomit monsters in a women's bathroom. I shove open the door and step inside.

This bathroom is even smaller than the men's. There's one sink, one toilet without stall walls, and Barb sitting on it with her pants around her ankles and my vomit monster in front of her shoes.

I freeze. She freezes. She's sitting on the pot, knees in, ankles out, trying to be a lady. Our eyes lock even though we both wish they hadn't. I see her body convulse up from her stomach to her mouth. She tries to say my name but can't. Her eyes plead but I don't know what for. She hucks again. Then again. Then she opens her mouth wide and the pointed legs of a vomit monster reach out over her lips. It pulls itself out and plops onto the tile floor.

Barb gasps for air. Hyperventilates. Turns pale. I aim the .45 and shoot twice. My stomach slug first. Hers next. They both burst like water balloons. The blood splatters on her clothes and face, but they're gone and she's okay.

I come up to her. It looks like she's about to faint, listing towards the bathroom wall, so I hold her. She's breathing like she ran a marathon. I put her head to my shoulder and say over and over again, "It's okay."

She breathes heavy and cries. Her torso bucks up from her stomach to her head, but not because she needs to vomit. Not now. It's those convulsions of a big cry. Eventually, she settles and asks me, "You too?"

"Yeah," I tell her. "You and me both. But we got each other now. We'll be okay."

Slaves to the Grind

Perfect coffee doesn't happen by accident. It takes fresh grounds, good equipment, and attention to detail. When I arrived at work that Monday, I had the equipment and a ration of beans there waiting for me, but I didn't know if I had the mental resilience to give the process the attention it needed.

My head fucking throbbed. Pulsing pain like a fat big brother sitting on your chest, keeping you from breathing. Hurt like a hangover. I wasn't hungover. Hadn't drank a drop all weekend. But still, that dry ach felt like sand poured directly into my eyeballs. I could barely keep my hands still as I put the beans onto my scale.

I shared my workstation with second and third shift, but they didn't mind my coffee setup on the back desk. The second shift guy had brought in one of those Keurig machines and let the third shift guy use it too. Neither of those twats were allowed to touch my setup.

I removed a few beans and watched the LED digits on the scale react. Twenty-five grams. Perfect. I used my hand and plowed them into the open top of my manual burr grinder.

Behind me, the computer pinged, telling me I had an email. An interruption. A distraction just when I didn't need it. But the supervisors required immediate responses, and I needed this job. God my head hurt. I needed the caffeine.

I spun around in the wheelie office chair to face the dual monitors and keyboard. The right monitor was dissected into four separate panels, each displaying the view of the four confinement rooms through closed circuit TV. Nothing seemed amiss in the confinement rooms. The left monitor displayed my work email. There was a big notification pop-up window. It was from the supervisors.

You forgot to punch in today.

"Oh for Christ's sake," I said. "Arcane fucking technology…"

Next to the door of the control station, just to the left of the computer, was an old fashion style punch clock and rack of time cards. There were only three time cards. One of me, one for Second Shift Guy, and one for Third Shift Guy. It's not like the supervisors were managing a factory full of laborers. We weren't even paid by the hour. I was monitored by closed circuit TV as much as the confinement rooms. They knew when I came and went. It was just something they insisted on. And it was too petty to really bitch about. So I snatched my time card out of its slot in the rack and jabbed it into the punch clock. The clock put holes in the cardstock, and I returned it to the slot. I spun back to the computer and hit the email "Reply" button.

Done.

Send. I spun back to the scale, grinder, kettle and hotplate. A momentary distraction. A hassle. A fifteen second sidetrack. Still, it frustrated me. Death by a million papercuts. Insanity by a thousand anxieties. My brain felt like it was being stabbed to death by a billion thumb tacks. Like someone was tattooing my cerebellum.

The beans were in the grinder. The grinder was set to the second lowest notch between Fine and Coarse. I cranked. The pops and cracks of the beans felt like puncture wounds to my brain, but the aroma was like morphine.

I only took a moment to hold the cup of grounds under my nose and inhale heaven. The smell was only a limbo anyway. True paradise came after the brew was on my tongue and all those happy little neurotransmitters leapt between synaptic clefts and eased the sensation of murder inside my mind. I poured the grounds into the dry French press. Then I popped the plastic cap off the jug of distilled water, filled the kettle and flipped on the hotplate.

"Oh yeah, babe. You know what I need," I said.

The coffee was the best thing about this job. The only good thing about this job.

I had to let the water get up to temp before I could press it. It was a process, I know. As impatient as my brain was, I was tempted by the automatic single-cup brewer my co-worker had next to my setup. The little plastic cups of knock-off flavors sat in a little basket next to the machine. The tinfoil cap of the cups boasted the name of that international coffee shop franchise who must not be named. Voldemort Coffee as far as I was concerned. Still, I could swap the used cup that was surely still in the machine for a fresh cup as fast as a Green Beret could swap machine gun magazines. The resulting beverage would soothe my caffeine migraine, sure, the same way a two-dollar hooker could get me off. But what about after the deed was done? Could I look at myself in the mirror? Would I give up making good coffee and just spend the rest of my life slumming through auto-brew machines and corporate drive-thrus? Could I ever love again?

I was mesmerized by the slow boil of the water. Tiny bubbles rose up from the bottom of the decanter. But what was the saying about a watched pot? I told myself there was work to be done and doing the work would help the water boil faster. I spun back to the monitors.

I checked the right monitor.

Room 1 held Experiment 1: a woman in a white walled room with a Rubix cube. Room 2 was occupied by Experiment 2: a man with a chess set. He had no one to play with but himself. But there he was with a bunk, an institutional sink and toilet combo, a small table, and a cheap chess set. The pieces weren't arranged per chess rules, nor were they set mid-game, pawns forward, the queen daring out into the fray, the king secured by rooks, none of that. If I had to guess, he was maybe playing checkers without any regard for which piece played which part. Or maybe he'd never played any game and only set the pieces on the board for his own hidden and purely aesthetic desires. Experiment 3 was the man in Room 3. He had a thick book of old poems. He used it to hide his face from the light in the room that stayed on between zero six and twenty-one hundred hours every day. Who knew if he ever read a verse of Tennyson or a single Shakespearean sonnet? I didn't. I didn't care. Room 4, of course, held Experiment 4: a woman, a big dollop of modeling clay, and a complete lack of skill in the field of sculpting. A couple of days ago she'd made a few Play-doh snakes and spheres. Since then, the clay sat on the small table between her bunk and bathroom while she paced from one wall to the other.

Five minutes to feeding time. I had to hit the "Meal Delivery" icon on the computer promptly at zero seven forty-five, or I'd get another piece of hate mail from the supervisors. Five minutes. Plenty of time to brew and enjoy my morning glory.

I spun back to my setup. The tiny bubbles had turned to big bubbles, the size of dimes and nickels. I flipped the switch off the hotplate and set the decanter on a hot pad. I set my kitchen thermometer into the water and watched that digital display. It had to cool. Two hundred degrees. It couldn't be off by more than a few degrees. I could taste the difference. Second and third shift guys could drink the swill and not know the difference, but not me. I enjoyed my coffee. I respected it. I knew the process and knew it's nuanced rewards. It didn't take long for the water to cool to two hundred. I readied the French press. Right when the digital thermometer blinked from 201 to 200, I poured the water over the grounds. I didn't fill the press. Just soaking the beans there. The full two cups of water would come a little later.

An alarm went off behind me. Not the standard email ping, but a squawking honking buzzer that crucifixed my temporal lobe like audio Roman Centurions.

"Motherfuckers," I swore involuntarily. Another spin in my chair generated vertigo in my fragile mental state. There was another pop-up window on the left monitor. Another email from the bosses.

Confinement breach.

I looked at the right monitor and saw that Experiment 3 had abandoned his lessons on Lord Byron and William Blake. Hell, he'd abandoned his whole damn room. I looked back at the email that had arrived as fast as the alarm, only muted by the constant hollowing from some unseen speaker imbedded in the ceiling.

"Confinement breach. No shit," I said.

I looked back at the French press and the soaking beans. Thirty seconds. That's how long the beans should soak before I add the rest of the water and start to press.

"Fuck!"

I left the control station and hammered down the metal grate stairway that led to the experiment floor. God damn job that never left me a moment's peace. God damn supervisors and their passive-aggressive observations and emails. God damn experiments.

"Hey!" I barked, loud, sharp, and commanding. "Get back in your room!"

Experiment 3 wore a hospital gown. All the experiments wore hospital gowns. He stood in the middle of the hallway lopsided and slow like an unmotivated zombie. His buzzed head and unresponsive eyes barely engaged me.

"I need help," he said, slow and uncoordinated. His lips moved to form the words with all the agility and dexterity of a mudslide.

"You know the deal," I told him. "You signed the papers. Get the hell back in your room before you get us both in trouble."

"I don't want..." he started to say.

I eased my aggressive posture. I came up to him and took him by the shoulders. I looked him in his limp eyes.

"Listen, man. This experiment is important. It's not my fault if you're bored out of your ever-loving mind. I'd be bored too. But you signed up for this shit and it's my job to make sure you stick to the deal," I talked with him. "Come on now. The poetry can't be that fucking bad. They had to keep it around this long for some reason. Let's be cool and get back in the room, okay?"

He didn't so much respond and he didn't resist. I turned him by the shoulders and guided him back through the open door and he dragged his dirty white socks across the linoleum.

"There you go. Just take it easy. You only got a little while longer," I said. "Just a few more days."

As soon as he was inside, I began easing the door shut behind him. I think I heard him ask what day it was, but the door was shut and locked before he finished his sentence.

"Crazy fucking experiments," I said and I double checked the deadbolt.

Fucking Third Shift Guy must have left it unlocked. First the bottle of bourbon under the desk and now this. The supervisors would hear about this. But these were fleeting thoughts. My real concern sat in two inches of quickly cooling water back in the control room.

I ran down the hall, grabbed the railing to powerslide around the turn and pumped my legs up each step like pneumatic pistons. I flung open the door to the control station, plopped my butt back in the chair and spun/rolled to my coffee setup.

How long had that taken? Was the water cold now? Was this cup ruined? Did I waste the only beans I had for today? I touched the decanter with my bare hand. Still hot. Maybe not ideal, but still okay. Who knew. Maybe I'd stumbled upon a new method to brew and achieved a cup that was an evolutionary leap from past cups. That's how genetic mutations sometimes worked. Maybe, just maybe, this mutation would be for the better.

I poured the rest of the decanter over the soaked beans inside the French press. That particulated steam that only fresh coffee makes rose up out of the decanter. I could almost see the microscopic airborne caffeine molecules rise up out of the French press. They filled my nasal passages and eased the throbbing ache behind my eyes. I picked up the lid and the plunger of the French press.

The email pinged again. So close.

"I swear to every god ever invented..." I spun in my chair and read the left monitor.

You're late on meal delivery. Timeliness is very important here.

"Timeliness. What about my time? What about my fucking coffee?" I asked. I don't know if they heard me. I don't know if they ever heard me. They never spoke to me over the speakers, and they never replied to emails either. One-way traffic only.

No use in arguing. Just another petty task in an endless line of petty tasks. I moved the computer's mouse and hovered the cursor over the "Meal Delivery" icon. Two clicks, and deep inside the building a series of conveyors and lifts came to work. Those unseen machinations did the actual work. They did the delivery. I just clicked the icon.

Not for the first time, I wondered why they even needed me. I was no computer coder, but I was sure that even I could design some program to put the meal deliveries on a timer. If timeliness was so god damn important, why leave it up to me?

These are things I'd never say out loud, not in here where the supervisors were always monitoring, and not outside where I was contracted to secrecy. I needed this job. After all, my coffee setup, from the fresh beans to the ceramic cup weren't mine. The company provided it all, just as they provided the Second Shift Guy with the Keurig, and I was beginning to suspect, they provided the Third Shift Guy with the bottle of bourbon under the desk.

I needed this job. I needed this coffee. This perfect, robust but sweet, rich but smooth, cup of coffee. I placed the lid over the French press and eased down the plunger. I'd sell my soul for what was left above the plunger's filter. Maybe I already had.

I poured my vice from the press into my cup. That aromatic steam that is so much more than steam rose up. Every one of those besieged neural receptors tingled with pleasure, no different than when the pain of a limb fallen asleep erbs in favor of sensation again. For me, this is what life smells like.

The French press was forgotten. I raised the coffee cup off the desk with both hands, careful not to spill a drop. Once I had it stabilized, I turned the chair and eased it towards the monitors so I could watch the experiments in peace while sipping my life's pleasure.

Cup came up to lips. Coffee rolled to tongue. Dopamine, serotonin, and endorphins loosen and traveled down axons. Another sip. Heaven. Fucking heaven. Those neurotransmitters reached the end of their axons and made that daring leap across the synaptic cleft. Already two sips in, I knew this feeling would fade, but not before it peaked around cup number two. Until then, until that restless numbing crash, I cherished every second.

The sensation! Those Folgers commercials could never do it justice.

Over the rim of my cup I watched the right monitor. Beige pureed food-stuff had appeared in each room. The experiments were scraping it off of the plastic trays that had slide through a slit in the wall. The slits had closed like doors in Star Trek and left the experiments alone with their slop. They ate it like competitors, shoulders hunched over their trays on the floor, as if one of them might bust into another's room and steal the meal.

Everyone has their vises. They had theirs; I had mine.

I closed my eyes and smelled. I raised the cup an inch from my lips when the alarm kicked back on. I jolted, all the wrong nerves firing for all the worst reasons. I came off balance in my chair. Coffee splashed up and landed on my shirt and my hands. It burned. I let out some noise that was less intelligent but more expletive than a swear word.

I held the cup away from me for a moment, betrayed by my closest love. When I realized it could burn me no more but was susceptible to more loss if I continued to handle it, I set it down next to the keyboard. The alarm still bayed overhead. I turned my attention to the monitors. The left one had a fresh email.

Confinement breach.

Again, no fucking shit.

The right monitor was where the action was. God damn Experiment 3 was loose. Again! How in holy hell did he… It didn't matter. This head case was going to go back to his room, or I would put him-

"What is he doing?" I asked no one. "What the fuck are you doing?"

He was turning the deadbolt on Room 4; that's what he was doing.

"No! You son of a bitch!"

My perfectly brewed cup of perfect coffee was abandoned on the desk. A god damn Shakespearean tragedy. Not that Experiment 3 knew anything about that with his god damn poetry book laying on the floor next to his slop tray!

I charged down the steps.

"Motherfucker, I told you to stay in your god damn-" I yelled, but no one was listening.

3 had unlocked 4, the sculptor who was the exact opposite of Michelangelo.

Nega-Michelangelo came rushing out of Room 4, screaming like a fucking banshee. The screams hadn't formed words yet, but Jesus Christ.

"No! Back in your rooms! You signed the fucking papers," I yelled as I ran towards them.

4 was running at me. We collided like linebacker and running back, or maybe two estranged lovers reunited, or the strangest case of the boy spotting his lost dog across a hay field. She knocked me on my ass and landed on top.

This experiment, this ragged raging woman hung her face over me, her ratted hair making a tunnel between my face and hers. Her drool strung from her lips down to my cheek. I was scared that if she peeled back her eyelids any further, they'd lose grip on her eyeballs, and those would come plopping down on top of me too.

Her banshee moans quickened enough to become recognizable words, like one of those pictures of long lines that, only when you look at it from a sharp angle turn into a secret legible message.

"Get us out of this hell!"

"Get off of me!" I yelled back.

Then Experiment 2 ran by us, he was barefoot and the back of his hospital gown was undone, giving me a great view of his cottage-cheese ass as he went.

"No!" I yelled again. Words were useless, as useless as those messages with the extra-long letters.

I rolled, turning me and 4 over so I could escape her. She clawed as I scattered off of her. She screamed, indecipherable again. As I scrambled away, I saw 3 unlock 1's room. Great. They were all out now. The psycho sculptor, the ignorant poet, the solo chess master and now...

1 came out of her room like a god damn SWAT team. She crossed the threshold, turned directly towards me, and pelted me with the Rubix cube. A real deadeye this 1. Fucking thing hit me square in the forehead. One of the little cubes popped off and clattered to the linoleum.

Still crawling away from 4's razor sharp talons, I watched as 2 made it to the one place they could not go: the exterior door.

"No! Get away from that door! I need this job!"

I ran up behind the man as he pulled on the handle. The door was locked from the outside, thank God, but he kept pulling and tugging on the handle, putting all his body weight behind each pull. The door wobbled and shook in its frame. 3 joined him, the zombie chess master who'd started all this. They both put their hands on the handle and were yanking together.

I almost knocked over 1 as I ran and she went to recover her Rubix cube/rubber bullet. I came up behind 2, his bare ass in full view, and grabbed him by the shoulders. I pulled him away, harder than he was pulling on the door handle. He spun away and fell. 3 and I turned face to face. I shoved him as hard as I'd ever shoved anyone before.

Had I ever shoved anyone before? Third graders shove other third graders. We were god damn adults. What was this nonsense?

"I said get back to your rooms!" I commanded them all. "This is my job! And being in your rooms is your fucking job. So go do your fucking jobs so I can do mine!"

"This place is a fucking prison!" 4 screamed at me from down the hall. She was still on her hands and knees, but she crawled towards me. Her eyes were locked with mine like she was Linda Blair. "We want out!"

"Out," 3 said.

"Let us go," cottage-cheese butt said from the floor.

1 said nothing, but she chucked that Rubix cube at me again. I ducked. It exploded in twenty six pieces against the door behind me. She didn't say a word, but I caught her drift.

"Listen. Listen, listen," I had to calm them down. Had to reason with them. "I need this job. You need this job. I've seen you. Watched you for how long now? You can't live out there. You need your meal delivery. You've always enjoyed that. You need it. And haven't I always been there to give it to you? Haven't I always done that for you? So do this for me. Go back to your rooms and we can all have what we want. What we need."

"It's slavery," said 4 coming closer to me again.

They were all coming closer to me now. Even cottage-cheese butt had pick himself up off the floor. He and 3 were grabbing at me, taking fists full of my shirt. 4, the banshee, the failed Michelangelo, she was on her feet and walking down the hall towards me. Her fingers were spread but curved, ready to shred me like a pork sandwich. She'd rip my eyeballs as loose as hers would be if she didn't fucking blink real soon.

"Slavery!" she screamed, spittle spraying out ahead of her like artillery before a cavalry charge.

The charge would come soon. She'd kill me. They'd rip the door off the hinges. I'd be fired and then no more…

That was it. We all had our vices.

I windshield wipered away their grabby hands. I had to shove again, had to put cottage-cheese ass right back down on his… ass. I got free of them, just as the bugles went off inside of 4's head and she started her Charge of the Mental Brigade. I ran for the staircase. She was right on my heels. I took the steps two at a time. When I got to the door I side-stepped and flung it wide open. It cracked her straight in the face. I didn't wait to see if it sent her tumbling backwards. I slipped inside the booth, slammed the door behind me and flipped the deadbolt.

The others were coming up the stairs now too. All four of them piled against the glass, pawing and pounding on it. Just as sure as they would have eventually busted through the door to the outside world, they'd bust down this door soon enough. The security glass wobbled in its casing with each slap and hammer fist.

My perfectly brewed cup of coffee was still sitting next to the keyboard. It was cold now. No steam. No aroma. Impotent and lame. I had no time to mourn.

I grabbed the computer mouse. I'm sure this was against protocol. I wasn't sure it would even work, but if it did, I would certainly get another email. I didn't care. I was out of options. I drug the cursor across the screen back to the "Meal Delivery" icon.

"Please god," I said and clicked twice.

The churning and spinning of the internal workings of the delivery machines was like a dog whistle to the experiments. They raised their snouts and turned their heads as if trying to find the source of a smell brought on by a stroke.

1 was the first to abandon the siege, the Rubix Cube sniper. Then 2 left, giving us all one more view of that gorgeous chunky ass as it jiggled down the steps. The conveyors and lifts grew louder and 4's eyes seemed to glaze over. She shoved off the door, plowed past 3 and then 2. 3 was the last to leave. The poetry hater. The escape artist. The freedom fighter. But we all have our vices. When he left, he made eye contact with me first.

He didn't speak, but it was clear he was trying to tell me something with his expressions.

I checked the right monitor. All the Star Trek doors opened and fresh trays of beige puree slid out, knocking aside the empty trays the experiments had just cleaned only a few minutes ago. They started filing back into their rooms, like cows at milking time.

I waited until they were all back in their rooms before I unlocked and cracked open the control room door. All quiet on the western front. I snuck down the metal staircase, as quiet as I could. I started with Room 1. I eased the door shut like a parent who'd just tucked in their kid. I flipped the deadbolt and went on to Room 2. I watched him eat from the tray to mouth and couldn't help but know it was going straight to his ass. The lock went click. Nighty night. Room 3. The poetry hating cause of all the mayhem. I locked him in.

"No!" I heard him call behind the door, but it was too late.

Room 4. The mound of clay was still a blob, the sculptor fascinated by a slightly less malleable medium now. I locked the last door, and that was that.

3 was pounding on the door as I walked past, still calling out. I double checked the lock. Then triple checked it. I even gave the door a pull myself. Locked tight. No more getting out today.

I carried myself back up the stairs to the control room. My legs stung from claw wounds left by 4. I had a welt on my forehead from 1's Rubix cube. I couldn't get the site of 2's pale ungulate butt cheeks out of my head everytime I closed my eyes and 3's last protest still rung in my ears.

Even worse than all that, my coffee was cold and ruined. I was out of beans to grind and the headache was coming back, worse than before. When I stepped through the door into the control room, I almost broke down in tears.

There on the back desk, freshly poured from a newly filled French press, was a steaming cup of perfectly ground, perfectly soaked, perfectly poured coffee. As I sat down, the little Star Trek door behind my setup slid shut. I wrapped my hands around the cup, and felt the heat. I inhaled and reveled in the particulate airborne coffee. All those happy chemicals went back to firing across those synaptic clefts. I put cup to lips and drank.

Heaven.

New Age Digital Hero

It's like my big brother said, why should we care if some person we'll never meet dies on the other side of the globe? If they wanted to live, maybe they shouldn't have done whatever it was that made them a target. The armies of the world knew what they were doing. They had their master plans. They just needed guys like my brother Mike to execute their plan.

Besides, it was the only way to really be alive. That's what Mike said. He said when you're directing an infantry bot, a drone tank or attack helicopter and you knew it wasn't just a sim but the real deal... That's what it's like to really live.

We'll never get the chance to fight wars and live lives like our great grandpas and grandmas. We didn't need humans to defend the pass at Thermopylae or flush out insurgents in Fallujah anymore. Nobody was out there storming the beaches of Normandy. The days of heroes and valor are gone. Our generation had left patriotism and nationalism in the history books. The closest we could get to service was our stations.

Truth be told, there was never any reason to have humans inside tanks. The weakest piece of the machine was the pressurized sack of blood and guts inside the turret. All the controls are digital. Nothing has been analog since the 21st century. Why not remote in? And why not put kids already trained by video games behind the controls?

So we toiled away, hoping some recruiter out there would take notice and we'd make the cut. Mike made it. He was getting missions almost every day now. The older kids said that when it was a real mission instead of a sim, it took a toll. I didn't prod him to talk about it. I'd see him shuffle out of his bedroom at 0600 and could tell by looking that he wasn't tired from just waking up. He'd been on mission through the night. Those mornings, and those mornings were coming more often than not lately, he wouldn't talk much. He looked gaunt and physically exhausted, even though he hadn't moved from his station all night.

Tuesday morning he came out of his room like that. Arms dangling as he walked instead of swinging. Eyes vacant and bagged. He wore underwear and nothing else. I didn't remember seeing his ribs through his skin before then. He sat down at the table with me and commandeered some milk and cereal. We ate in silence.

After he slurped the milk from the bottom of the bowl he looked up at me. His hair was a mess. His eyes were bloodshot. When he spoke his lips barely moved. I was so proud of him.

"I leveled up last night. They gave me a tank company. If this goes well I could end up controlling a jet fighter any day now," he said. "What level are you at in the sim?"

"89," I said.

"Better work harder than that if you ever want to fly. I was at 120 by the time I was your age."

He got up and dumped his bowl into the sink. Then he shuffled back into his room. Whether he'd go to bed and accept another mission I couldn't guess.

120. One hundred and twenty. Damn. Would I ever make it to 120? Right then I doubted I'd ever get a real mission, never mind command a tank company or fly a jet.

I put my bowl in the sink. I may have forgotten to put the milk away. There was more important things to worry about than warm milk. I had work to do.

Kids at school told rumors of operators getting picked up below 100 if an army saw what they liked in the sim. Work your units just right and and some backwater country might give you a shot with an infantry team. You just had to have the skills and get lucky. 89 wasn't so low that it was unthinkable for a recruiter to take a chance on me. After all, infantry bots weren't *that* expensive.

I went into my room and looked at my station. Controllers, monitors, a headset and seat. Empty pop cans on the floor and crumbs in the keyboard. It wasn't much but it was my path to the rest of the world. Honor. Glory. Victory. If any of that was attainable for my generation, my station was my only means to get it. I sat down, plugged in, logged on and set the difficulty meter to the max.

The sim gave me a building clearing mission. Take out a sniper. Civilians present. Possibly mined. Three infantry teams had failed before. I was going in alone. It was just a sim, but you never knew when the recruiters were out there watching your every move. If I pulled this off, who knew how many levels they might bump me up?

I spawned in an urban back alley. I checked my onscreen compass and found my target. 300 meters away. Four stories up in an apartment complex. The alley opened up into a town square that sat between me and my target. There was a side street that would take me around the square to the side of the target building. It was the obvious answer. To take out a sniper you had to stick to the shadows and work around his flanks. That's what they expected you to do. They wanted me to go that way. I didn't see any movement from the side street, but something about how still it sat told me it was a trap. Soldiers, mines and ambushes waited for me down that way, no doubt about it.

I scanned the town square. There was another building next to the apartment where the sniper laid in wait, a retail store with offices on the second and third floor. It was closer than the apartment building. If I rushed the apartment I was sure the sniper would pick me off. But if I moved quick and in a direction he didn't anticipate, maybe I could make it to the store front.

Victory belongs to the bold. I readied my rifle and planted my feet. A quick jerk on the controls and my infantry bot charged into the square.

I saw the muzzle flash come from an apartment window. I marked it as rounds impacted against the cobblestone square all around me. Mike had showed me how to serpentine while he was still playing sims. It took skill to do it right, but I had the trick down. My infantry bot zigged and zagged, and just when the sniper thought he had my pattern down, I cut for the retail store.

His bullets chased me, always just a meter or less behind me. Five meters from the building I triggered my bot to hurdle through the storefront window. Its titanium-alloy frame shattered the glass into a thousand bits. Digital bits sure. The titanium-alloy was really made of just 1s and 0s too, but it felt real to me.

The retail building was empty. I moved through abandoned product and the detritus of society collided with war. I found the fire stairs and made my way to the roof.

My bot busted through the locked hatch and climbed to the top of the building. Down below, I could hear enemy soldiers barking orders as they sprinted across the square, trying to reset their defenses. They had been waiting for me in those side street traps and now had to reconfigure their formation. I wasn't about to give them time to recompute a new plan.

The corner room where I'd marked the sniper was only an alley away. A ten meter leap maybe. I wasn't sure a bot could do it, but I needed something to catch the recruiter's eyes. I needed to get noticed. I replanted my feet, breathed in real deep and slammed the controls forward at full speed. When I reached the ledge, I dove headfirst.

It was too far, I was sure of it. I was about to experience what it would be like to drop a thousand pound hunk of metal twenty meters off a building.

Digital titanium-alloy finger caught digital brick window ledge. The bot's grip held. It dangled four stories up, just outside the target's window. Yes!!!

I maneuvered the bot into a quick pull-up and vault. More digital broken glass. The target was there in the room. A human sitting behind a table with a sniper rifle rested there aimed into the square. A digital human, sure, but he looked as real as me or Mike in the sim. All the same, I drew my gun and scrambled his 1s and 0s.

I threw off my headset and fist pumped the air. And just like that I was back in me and my brother's cruddy apartment. Oh well. In here, at this station, I was a hero.

I saw on the screen that my leveled bumped from 89 to 93. I started fist pumping again. I thought of telling Mike about it, but there was a good chance he was sleeping. And he had real fights. I didn't want his accomplishments to drown out my small victory.

93. 93! I was getting there. Seven more and I'd be officially eligible for recruitment. Maybe I could make it. Maybe I could command infantry teams, tank companies, fighter jets... Hell, maybe I could even command squadrons of jets. There was nothing that said my big brother had to over-shadow me my whole life.

Then I looked at my screen and saw an unfamiliar message there.

It looked scrambled, like it had broken through some firewalls to get to me. All the same, the text was clear and plain to read.

SECRET MESSAGE FOR:

It said my name.

YOU HAVE BEEN SELECTED TO OPERATE AN INFANTRY BOT IN A COVERT OPERATION. THE TARGET IS AN ENEMY OPERATIVE RESPONSIBLE FOR SIGNIFICANT DAMAGES TO FRIENDLY FORCES. YOUR IMMEDIATE ACTION IS REQUIRED FOR THE SAKE OF FREEDOM AND CIVILITY. DO YOU ACCEPT THIS MISSION?

YES/NO

This was it. I was being recruited. It wasn't just boy's bathroom rumors. They liked my style and my skills. They needed me. I had to tell Mike.

My cursor blinked between the YES and the NO. The words IMMEDIATE ACTION seemed to lock my eyes in place. Would they pass me over if I hesitated? What if I did tell Mike but then failed the mission?

Victory belongs to the bold. I sat back down, plugged back in and selected YES.

The mission was a quick hit and run. The target was inside an apartment building, not unlike my last sim. But sims were a thing of the past. From here forward, it was real. No more 1s and 0s. Take out an high-level operator. Watch for enemy troops. Avoid collateral damage when possible. Eliminate the target at all costs.

I spawned inside an airborne troop transport. Air insertion. Cool. Just me and one other bot. It looked at me.

"First time?" another voice asked. This was a human voice. Another operator somewhere in the world. He sounded young, maybe as young as me, so I was honest.

"Yeah. First time," I said.

"Me too," the operator said.

The countdown to drop was onscreen. Ten seconds. We readied our bots. I turned to my comrade.

"Good luck," I said to him.

"Thanks. You too," he said back.

The countdown reached zero and we dropped from the bottom of the plane. The transport was gone. I couldn't spot my teammate. I sailed through clouds and smog. A city laid below. My onscreen compass showed the target's location. My altimeter told me he was 1000 feet below. I adjusted the bot's thrusters so I'd come down right on top our target, that sorry SOB of an operator. I spotted a nice flat rooftop where I could land. As I cruised through the day time air, I saw my partner coming in for the same building.

We slowed our descent and came to rest on the pea-rock roof. Upon touchdown, I killed the thrusters and let the dust settle and clear from my screen. I scanned the area and found a doorway leading to a staircase. My partner was already unclamping his weapon from its mount and headed for the door.

"Wait," I said. My last sim seemed custom made for this real world mission. Something told me the expected way to the target was a trap. Mined maybe. An ambush for sure.

I went over to the roof ledge and looked down. A city intersection with a hundred passing cars sat below. A city block more modern than the sim's but identical to a million city blocks I'd walked through in real life. The target was two stories down.

I cycled through my bot's inventory and found a grapnel hook and cable. These real bots were fully stocked.

"What? What is it?" my partner asked.

"We can go through the window. Bypass their defenses. Why go in the way they expect when we can go straight to the target?" I said.

He peeked over the edge. "I guess if we fall, it's not like we die, right?"

I made my bot give his bot a friendly slug in the shoulder. "Victory goes to the bold."

We clamped our grapnel hooks into the ledge and measured the radius to the target's window. A ten meter jump should swing us right through the glass. Real glass this time. Real titanium-alloy too.

When I set my feet into the pea-rock rooftop it felt just like in the sim. Tactile stimulation. True to life graphical interface. Stereophonic sound. But this wasn't a sim. This was reality. I hit my controls and the bot charged for the ledge. I jumped out the full ten meters and drew the cable attached to the grapnel taunt. Gravity did the rest. I swung down in an arc into an apartment window.

When that titanium-alloy infantry bot smashed through the apartment window it was like the world exploded. The sound was a thunderclap. The impact was an earthquake. I felt it both in my chest and feet. Not my bot's feet. *My* feet. This was more than sim-real. This was...

I took off my headset.

A towering scuffed up greasy seven foot tall infantry bot was standing in my bedroom. Its hull was marred by a hundred previous battles. Its stenciled-on foreign words were scrapped and ineligible. The thing was poised in a battle ready stance, its huge hands held a thick barreled machine gun that messed like oil and sulfur. My window was shattered and so was the window frame and a part of the wall where the metallic beast couldn't fit through. Air blew in through the hole and flutters my curtains. The bot seemed to pump slowly up and down like it was taking massive heaving breaths. I know it didn't breathe because it didn't need to. Operators breathed. I breathed.

I looked at my screen and looked through the eyes of the beast. I'd assaulted my own god damn apartment. Only I wasn't the target. It was Mike.

Another blast of thunder crashed into my brother's room next door. It was my partner. He was executing my plan. He was beating me to the target.

I screamed for him to stop as I ran out of my bedroom, not on robotic titanium-alloy feet, but little human feet wrapped in cotton socks. I burst through Mike's door precisely when my partner took his killshot.

Mike was a gory mess, still plugged into his station but now mindless, useless and dead. On his screen I saw a jet fighter nose downward into a tailspin over some far away foreign city.

The infantry bot that had killed him loomed over his corpse with a smoking barrel and an apathetic face.

The voice of my partner came through a speaker implanted in the bot. "Sorry kid. If he wanted to live, maybe he shouldn't have made himself a target."

Somewhere far away, a kid I'd never meet in real life hit a button that retracted the infantry bot's cable. The monster was pulled outside through my brother's window and back towards my roof.

On screen, my brother's jet crashed into an oil refinery and the screen went blank for just a moment. Then text appeared:

MISSION FAILED.

Manna for the Great Machine

I stood before the face of God, under His towering monolith of earthly presence, and uttered blasphemy.

"Fuck you."

God didn't hear, at least He showed no signs of taking offense. He churned on, a million pistons, cogs, sprockets, bellows, and pressure tanks all working in perfect synchronization. God, the Great Machine, was here before us humans, would be here after, had spawned the millions of lesser machines all around, and surely thought of me as insignificant.

Father Michael did his best to nurture our faith, mine needing more nurturing than most. He reminded us that the Great Machine worked at His own accord with His own purpose. We soft, flesh-made, imperfect humans were blessed to live near His presence. He gave us manna to eat, rods for warmth, and lesser machines to study His holy ways and provide for us.

I held a small chunk of a shattered plutonium-239 fuel rod in my gloved hand. It pulsed a glowing green iridescence. The hood of the radiation suit hung down my upper back. I wanted God to hear me when I told Him off. Besides, now that I was out of the reactor, the radiation was nominal. After all, I'd soon put the rod in a potbelly stove to heat our home and cook our food.

The Decommissioning Pit wasn't far from where I stood, just a few steps forward, just below the face of God. A dozen metal-shredding rollers and cones covered in claws and spikes churned deep inside the pit. The Great Machine gave us life but made us pay for it with death. There was a balance to His actions. An output equal to the input.

I put the plutonium in a small case and turned my back on God. As I walked away, I dragged behind a hoisted fist and a raised finder. He took his. I'd take mine.

#

As bold and brash as I felt at the pinnacle of the Great Machine, staring into the face of God and defying His rule, I felt like a little girl and a coward on the way back home. No human eyes had seen me on top of the Great Machine. Not Father Michael. Not my husband Howard. If they had seen me, they'd chastise me endlessly. They'd shame me. Let me know just how stupid of a woman I was. Urge me to recant and prostrate myself to earn back God's favor. And worse than that, they'd fear for my soul.

They were true believers. God had never spoken to them, never strayed from His divine rhythm and purpose, never hesitated in His perfect eternal course of cause and effect. His cams would move the valves. The valves fed the combustion chambers which pressurized the tanks. His release valves would maintain the precise pressure to stabilize the tanks. He would generate output regardless of our praise to Him or my secret blasphemy. But they believed all the same.

After all, the Great Machine gave us the lesser machines. And besides us sparse humans in this eternal metropolis, there were only machines. It had always been this way. Sure, there were rumors of accident times, of men ruling of machines, but these were no doubt made-up fantasies.

I wish it was that easy for me. I would have prayed for faith to come to me as easy as it seemed to embrace others if only I believed in prayer.

On my walk back home, I was careful to not step on the metallic bugs that skittered across the alleyway. A steel snake chased some of the larger bugs down an open pipe. Above, a sparrow clinked its wings against a girder that stretched across the alleyway. It sang a perfect one thousand hertz tone. When another human crossed a perpendicular alley ahead of me, our eyes met for only a moment before the man went his own way.

I came to the steel bridge that crossed the city's diesel canal. A gigantic spiral cog rolled upstream along its submerged track. When it was gone, the bridge began lowering down from its gantries high above. When it rested level with the alley, I walked across and noticed the streams of oil floating on top of the river of diesel. There was a leak somewhere upstream. No doubt the priests would find it, patch it, and thinking nothing of a flawed deity.

I thought of it, even if they didn't.

#

Home was the old housing of a lesser machine, long forfeited by the Great Machine and gifted to Howard and me. I spun the dog lever and unlocked the hatch. The heavy door fell inward on rusted hinges. It was dark and cold inside. The dim light of a clouded night sky did little to penetrate the dark. I stepped inside and pulled out the broken bit of plutonium rod.

When I held the rod above my head, it shone its sickly green light about a meter past my nose. It was enough. I moved under the green light through our humble abode to the stove, opened the lead door, and tossed the plutonium inside. It warmed the stove almost immediately and heated the filaments inside the stove even faster. The filaments conducted the heat away from the stove to a few bulbs hung from the ceiling. The bulbs slowly grew amber and bright.

"Welcome home," Howard said.

I turned and saw him bundled up in a blanket in the corner of our home. He looked pale. It was cold inside that old iron housing.

"You scared me."

"I put a pot of manna on the stove," he said. "I threw our old rod out. It wasn't even glowing anymore. If you hadn't brought that new rod home, our dinner would have been cold."

"Shouldn't be long now."

I looked at the pot on the stove. The manna was a beige paste, excreted from a lesser machine close to the Great Machine. Maybe it was from the Great Machine. Hard to tell where one mechanism ended and the next began.

"How was your trip to the pinnacle?" Howard asked. "You saw the face of the Great Machine." His voice was monotone, an effect the priests encouraged as a means to mimic the machines. It was a creation of their imagination. An idea of what God might sound like if He ever spoke. We should all aspire to be more like the machines as a way to show our reverence to God, our divine example of engineered perfection.

I tried to talk like them. I was never any good at it.

"Fine. There were plenty of rods, still glowing hot. I just had to pick one about the right size for our stove. I saw a man on the way back. I think some oil might be leaking into the diesel river."

"The Great Machine provides," Howard said. Flat. Emotionless. Contrite for his human-ness. "If there is a leak, I'll let Father Michael know. We will do our best to be worthy supplicants and worship God through our labor. It is good that He provides us with repairs to glorify Him."

"All hail the Great Machine," I said by rote. Howard said the name. To not hail when the name was mentioned was blaspheme, and that was best done in private.

We ate our manna, warm and electric in our mouths and stomachs. Then we slept. The jade glow of the rod shone through the dampers on the stove. We lay spooned together on the small cot in the corner. In the dark, I was isolated with my doubt and guilt.

There was no need for the sin I'd committed that day. There was no product of it or output gained by it. It was a stupid and childish act. The Great Machine had provided. I had warmth in my belly to prove it.

It was just that God was so muted and silent. The Great Machine provided, but in the long laborious days and the restless rumbling nights, He brought no comfort or intervention to make the next day any more satisfying than the last. We had nothing to look forward to than this, and beyond this, only the inevitable decay of our imperfect bodies.

During Decommissioning Ceremonies, we'd gather on top of the pinnacle, just below the face of God, and Father Michael would preach. He'd bolt on his holy metal vestments so as to be closer to God, and he'd tell us how we were inferior to the machines. We were flawed where they were precise but similar in design. The machines had bellows. We had lungs. The machines had steel scaffolds. We had our brittle bones. The machines had pumps and tanks. We had hearts and vessels. God had fuel and oil. We had manna and blood.

When we succumbed to our human flaws, we'd feed the Great Machine, and He would output in greater ways for having consumed our soft biological fuel.

I could feel my weakness. Daily, I observed God's strength. It was undeniable. The evidence of His divinity was constant.

Still, there was a part of me that wanted to see what it would take to halt His functions. To kill Him. If I shoved something larger and hard enough inside the shredders down in the depths of the Decommissioning Pit...

I hid the thought as soon as it was conscious. God saw our thoughts. Why were these moments of weakness so ready-made for my mind? My boldness turned to shame.

Tomorrow would be another day. I'd face it in a positive light. Howard and Father Michael found joy in their commitment to the Great Machine. They were serene. Happy. If I killed these sinful and flawed ramblings, perhaps I could achieve the nirvana they'd so easily found. I had to be better, if not for myself than for Howard. I loved him.

I closed my eyes.

#

Sleep came easily with the plutonium. Arousal was more difficult. It came with moans and slobbers. Perfect examples of our human frailties.

The plutonium rod still burned inside the stove and had turned the house into a sweat box. The glowing filaments of the light bulbs still burned, but daylight seeped through the cracks in the hatch door. An oval shine pierced into the dark housing.

"Howard. Howard, it's morning."

He was slower to wake up than I was. Our fleshy indecisive brains were lacking lubrication. Our bodies resisted action.

"Come on. Get up. You were going to meet Father Michael and tell him about the leak."

"He grumbled, "There's no leak. God is perfection."

"God makes room in His perfection for our labor," I quoted the texts as I checked to see what was left on the stove of the manna. It had been cooked into flakes. I chipped some away from the pot and set them aside. Breakfast. "The Great Machine has made room in His perfection for me today. There were some belts in the timing system that was squealing when I visited yesterday. I thought I'd grease them."

"His output is our opportunity," Howard quoted another verse. "And we are humbled by His glory."

I slipped on a set of threadbare coveralls. I wouldn't need the radiation suit today. The plutonium rod should last for a month.

"Will you get more manna on the way home?"

"Yes," he said. "If the leak is upstream, I'll walk right by the dispensary."

All hail the Glorious Spigot of Gruel, I thought but didn't say. Why should I? I was going to be a good girl today.

#

My day of labor searching for zerks and pumping the small hand-held grease gun brought me into a narrow crawl space, somewhere in the foundations of the Great Machine. There, I found a rat.

It was broken, and I never saw a broken rat before. Its back leg had come loose and couldn't paw forward. So it lay lopsided on the steel grate, scraping but not moving forward. I picked up the tiny creature. Its thin sharp claws cut into my fingers as it tried to get away, but it was my penance for my behavior yesterday.

"God makes room for our labor in his Perf—"

The rat sank its steel fangs into my finger. I squealed and dropped the creature. Blood leaked from four dots in my finger. My teeth ground together and before I could stop myself, I raised up my heavy boot and slammed it down on the maimed rat. It crunched under the rubber sole.

"Oh God, what have I done?"

I slid my boot to the side, and the output of my actions was clear.

#

The wind blew across the pinnacle and I shivered under the thin layer of coveralls. The face of God had something like eyes glowing with the same green energy as the plutonium rods. A long lateral vent running along the bottom of the visage looked like a solemn mouth but never spoke a word. Below the face of God was the Decommissioning Pit.

I looked down into His churning maw and my thoughts were fixed on my sin. Last night's blasphemy and this morning's assault. Could I be saved now? How much more could the Great Machine tolerate before his judgment came down on me?

The rat was in my hand, busted and lifeless. Such a small action, yet with permanent results. If I could do that with just my boot, what would it take to bring God's eternal machinations to a halt? How big was the chunk of cast iron that would be able to crush back against the threshers inside the pit?

How many pilgrims came here to feed Him? How much would He eat before He was satisfied? Fuel rods. Vats of diesel and gasoline. The husks of innards of lesser machines. Our human dead. God ate everything. Greedily. His waited in constant motion for the next Decommissioning Ceremony. Who were we to deny Him?

I threw in the rat. It bounced off the sides of the chute, a delay before the inevitable unchangeable destiny. The shredders devoured the rat in a half-second. A flash of torn aluminum and airborne sparks. Then the thing was below the shredders and in the bowels of the rumbling towering God. A glorious end for a worthy machine we humans could only hope to emulate.

I turned to leave God to his functions. And as if He was waiting for me to break away, He dislodged an entire section of the city off its tracks.

From the mechanical peak, I saw the entire city. Several buildings not far from the diesel canal issued up dust and debris into the choked sky. Rooftops sunk as if there was suddenly no foundation underneath them. Various tanks and reservoirs ruptured and gushed fire. A huge spindle dislodged and toppled sideways. The foundations quaked under the Great Machine and by default, me.

"Howard."

It was a long way from the pinnacle. I shuffled as fast as I could. Spiral stairs poured me out onto ramps and then a counter-balanced dumb waiter descended me down to alley-level.

I stumbled and almost fell under my impatient and imperfect legs. Howard had most certainly gone to investigate the oil leak that tainted the diesel supply. If he was there when the superstructure had collapsed…

As I ran to the site, the dust of mortar filled the air and plumed along the alley-level like the breath of God Himself. I ran through it, coughing and blind as I went. When my foot hit the first brick, I fell onto the piles of rubble.

"Howard! Howard!"

Other humans were converging on this wreckage, struggling to figure out how and why our God had brought this upon us. They couldn't make sense of what had motivated the Great Machine to do this, but I knew. Even before I found Howard, I knew God had done this to equal the output of my sin.

Howard wasn't far into the rubble. Others had found him too. Father Michael was there, leering over his exposed torso protruding from the mass of twisted metal and cinder block. The priest, not yet in his metallic holy vestments, was reciting verses from the text.

Howard was leaking the frailest of our human components: blood.

"We have been engineered in the same design as the Holy One. Our creation is an ode to divinity. Our design a tribute to His great glory. We live to serve. We die to fuel," Father Michael was saying, not in a holy monotone pace, but so rushed the words almost sounded like nonsense.

It was another sin; I knew it, but I couldn't listen to the old lessons anymore. I grabbed the father by his shoulders and ripped him away from my Howard.

He was out of his senses, broken in a way that no lesser machine ever could be. Permanently on that all-too-human edge between awake and asleep. Unintelligent. Without purpose or design. Babbling. Overwhelmed with that wholly imperfect and human experience that was pain.

"Howard, don't be like this. It should have been me. It should have been me. I... I blasphemed. I murdered."

His eyes rolled about. His words were just consonants and ragged inhalations. His eyes rolled in every direction except anywhere near mine.

"No no no. You have been faithful. You have been pious. You..."

...are dead, I thought but didn't say. I just knew it when his eyes stopped rolling and his lungs stopped bellowing out those moans and convulsions. The green glow from down his throat dimmed, and the Great Machine took him from me.

Father Michael did what he could to comfort me. He really tried. I wasn't listening. Not to him. Not to the constant white noise of the millions of lesser machines grinding on all around us. Not to the perfectly pitched sparrows singing their tone around us. I alone was a machine whose cams had slipped on the shaft. I alone was malfunctioning.

"Enough of that now, my child," Father Michael whispered behind my ear. He hooked me under the armpits and lifted me away from my Howard. "It is time he is decommissioned."

Other men who had been searching through the rubble now came around either side of us. They cleared away the broken bricks and metal scraps until he was unburied. When they hoisted him up, I saw his head loll back, eyes open and skyward, parts of his closes wet with leaked fluid. I couldn't see the details of his injuries, could see exactly how he died. My eyes leaked and blurred my vision. I was crying out, loud and raw. So unmachine-like of me. This was the manifestation of my sin. My imperfection. My unbalance. My sin. I was impious in my passion. I was irredeemable.

Father Michael led the men carrying Howard towards the Great Machine. As they went, they chanted, "We live to serve. We die to fuel." The Decommissioning Ceremony would begin immediately.

#

Up there on the pinnacle, the countenance of God was unchanged. The Great Machine looked down, stoic and stern, as responsive as cold cast iron on an anvil. Below Him and before me was the Decommissioning Pit. The pit spoke, but only in waves of carbon-on-steel screeching, a system lacking lubrication.

The men laid Howard at the foot of God, at the brink of the pit. I crumbled to my knees at his side, a thick screen of lubricates pouring from my eyes and clouding my sight. The pallbearers averted their faces from me and God alike as they backed away. Somewhere behind me, Father Michael was preparing himself for the service, donning his holy vestments, piece by cast iron piece. Flesh was imperfect, but by bolting on the chassis of a machine, he could his humanly best to mimic the Great Machine perfect design. I didn't watch him assemble the vestments. My face was pressed against the deck of the pinnacle, but I heard him bolt on the last pieces. Then, heavy boot after heavy iron boot, I heard him approach through the mourners and towards me and Howard.

The clanking footfalls reverberated through the deck and into my flawed brain. There was so much single boot could do.

The congregation chanted from the texts. "We live to serve. We die to fuel. We pray so one day we may have mechanical worth. Let our human frailties be purged from our chassis and fuel the perfection of God."

Father Michael clunked forward in his vestments, stopping next to me. He put a dense metal glove on my shoulder. "Rise, my child. Today is a blessing. Only in death may we aspire to become divine. Your Howard can now be greater than any of us here still breathing."

"We live to serve. We die to fuel," the supplicants chanted. "Only in death may we aspire."

I put my weak feet under me and stood on uncertain legs. Father Michael was there to stabilize me. He had the advantage of being covered, neck to toe, in his thick metal chassis. It encased him in a dull dark gray cast iron housing. Bits of plutonium-239 were affixed to his chest. He was more God-like this way, dressed as a machine. He held me up against his metal chest, and I felt the warmth radiating from the plutonium rods. We stood over Howard, the side of my head against Father's chassis, turned to see the face of the Great Machine looking down on us.

Somewhere across the city, there was another collapse. A massive transmission seized up and slipped. The motor that it fed torqued loose from its mounting bolts and fell to the ground. Distal components broke free and busted apart. There were screams, warbling and panicked and full of erroneous human emotion. More would be coming to this place soon.

Doom was coming to our metropolis, and we ignored it. Or maybe I just hid my lust for it.

"No need for sorrow, my child," Father Michael said. "We are all like gears set by the Great Machine. We each grind for as long as we can until the day comes when He offers us rest. But you are blessed more than all the rest of us. You've been gifted this opportunity to sacrifice to God someone you hold so dearly. Speak, my child. Beseech the Great Machine for his blessings, and on this day He will hear you."

A flight of birds rose up from behind the face of God. As they swirled up to the heavens, they emitted their thousand-cycle tones, and it was as if the Great Machine was greeting me for the first time.

I lifted my countenance to look Him in the eyes and spoke.

"Fuck you."

The piecemeal bolted-on holy vestments were heavy. Too heavy for me to move on my own. Even Father Michael strained to walk in them. Thankfully, I had Howard to help me. His body laid just between us and the Decommissioning Pit, a soft and inferior curb, but enough of a curb to topple the giant metal suit and the man with his arms around me inside of it. I twisted, pulled, and fell over Howard, backward and hanging onto Father Michael with every ounce of strength.

The pit was deep. We plummeted together, him in shocked silence, me in vengeful glee. We spiraled while embraced, he being heavier than me. I clung to him. We had nothing else to hold on to but each other. Well, maybe he had his faith. The last rotation brought him underneath me. The metal suit slammed into the threshing drums. The spikes and metal teeth spun inward, digging into the holy vestments and Father Michael's flesh inside. Metal-carbide blades sparked. Axles groaned. The spindles bound and bucked. Belts snapped. Bearings ground and smoked. Father Michael was screaming but the noises of the shredder were louder. I rode on top of the Father and felt every jolt and buckle as the Great Machine did its best to digest him. I prayed He choked on him.

Sparks popped around us. The walls and spindles and foundations rattled. Smoke filled the pit. Humans wailed. Was one of them me? No. I'd said my peace, and The Great Machine had heard what I had to say.

Solo Pursuit

The girl from Outer Space raced down the frozen highway, and Sheriff Marty gave chase.

There were procedures for calling off a high speed chase. Policies. Considerations of public safety. Officer safety. Safety of the suspect. These were fleeting thoughts in Sheriff Marty's mind as he urged the speedometer of his V8 Ford Interceptor past a hundred miles an hour.

Too fast. One patch of ice could kill him and the suspect, but he suffocated those

As he tried to justify his actions, he repeated the clichés in his head, *Not this one. Not this time. She isn't getting away from me.*

A quarter mile ahead of his push bumper, an old Chevy Monte Carlo ripped down the narrow county highway, railed on either side by ice packed shoulders and ditches filled with old plowed snow. The roads were dangerous. The suspect, a kid who liked to steal cars, wasn't dangerous as long as she wasn't being chased. The decision to continue the pursuit, Sheriff Marty was reluctant to admit, wasn't rational, and none of the hardboiled cop-show lines did much to convince him otherwise. He tried them anyways, as if repeating lies often enough would make them truths.

Not on my watch.

Then, closer to home and less a lie, *I won't lose you like I lost Hannah.*

But it wasn't Hannah driving the Monte Carlo. It was Winona, a native girl from the rez and a troubled family. Winona had never met Hannah, and never would now, but he couldn't help but think of his daughter every time he saw this car thief.

He picked up the girl this morning, a Jane Doe, hauled her to jail, questioned her, and had her scheduled to see the judge on Monday.

But it was a Jane Doe driving the Monte Carlo. Not Hannah.

He'd picked up her up, hauled her to jail, questioned her, and had her scheduled to see the judge on Monday. He had her put away. And yes, when she inexplicably disappeared from her cell in the basement, he was instantly angry. He spotted her through his office window breaking into the Monte Carlo in the impound lot behind the station. Thin frame, black hair cut short, an unathletic gate running through the lot. By the time he was outside, she'd rammed the stolen car through the chain-link gate and the Chevy was spinning its tires through the slush and ice. He raced out of his office to his squad car, leaving his cold coffee and rationale behind.

But there was something more than a sense of justice or duty that propelled him down the highway after her.

He gave his squad car a little more gas and the needle moved to a hundred and ten. High speeds were suicide on these roads. He'd seen enough crash scenes to know the risk. Still, he pursued her. He only had to stay on her a while longer.

Sheriff Marty picked up the radio mic. "Car Two, Car One, over."

"Car Two here, boss." The voice of Eddie, his single deputy. This far north, he was lucky to have the budget for the two of them. Roseau County, the next department over, had one sheriff, one car, one jailer, one clerk, and zero deputies.

"Ready for intercept?" Sheriff Marty said.

"Almost. I'm coming up on the intersection now, boss."

"Us too. Hurry," was all Sheriff Marty said before tossing the mic aside and putting both hands on the wheel.

There were curves ahead as they came around Long Lake. In these conditions, the slightest turn could send a car fish-tailing into the snow. He watched the Monte Carlo's brake lights flicker. The driver, his female car thief, feathered the gas and counter-steered as the back tires slipped sideways. She was good. A far better driver the most kids her age.

He gained on her, but only a little. As long as Eddie got the spike strips out in time he wouldn't need to catch her, just keep her in sight.

"Come on, come on," he muttered.

It wasn't just that this nineteen year old girl from town had broken out from his jail and re-stolen a car from his in-pound lot right out from under his nose. It wasn't only because of how much she reminded him of his Hannah. It wasn't just that she'd been a good kid up to about six months ago when she found her sudden interest joy rides. What was the saying about cats and curiosity?

"I'm an alien," she told him when he took her statement in his office.

"You're a what?" Marty asked. She was native Sioux. Her family had been tribe members since anyone bothered to keep record and had lived on the rez since the US government had put them there. She was about as un-alien as they come.

"I know I don't look it," she said. "But this isn't my body. And I'm starting to outgrow the disguise. They say it happens not long after puberty."

"What do you mean 'alien'? Like..." He pointed to the ceiling and made a twirling motion with his finger. The unfinished sentence would have listed off flying saucers, laser guns, cattle mutilations...

She didn't make him go on. She just nodded politely with her hands cuffed and folded tightly in her lap. She fixed her eyes on his and he didn't break contact. When she blinked, Marty noticed something different. It was almost as if when she opened her eyelids, she peeled open her eyeballs too and for a moment showed Marty what was behind them: Something black and restless. Then the black disappeared and she lowered her head.

The Interceptor and Monte Carlo approached another long shallow curve. Marty watched her work the steering, keeping the Monte Carlo out of the ditch. A half-second later, he was massaging the Interceptor through the icy highway right behind her. The intersection and Deputy Edwards was just ahead. Marty slowed down and gave the Monte Carlo some space.

They came around another bend in the road. Marty saw the intersection, saw Car Two, saw Eddie standing at the open truck with the spike strips still rolled up in his hands, gawking at the oncoming chase. The Monte Carlo blasted through the intersection, stop sign, undeployed spike strip, and right past Eddie. He stood there mouth-breathing with the spike strip still in hand as Marty left him behind.

A few seconds later, Eddie was on the radio, wanting to know which intersection he should tried to get to next, as if Marty had a guess and as if Eddie could drive fast enough to get ahead of them. It was pure coincidence the chase had headed in Eddie's direction from the onset. Marty swore at the radio mic as it laid in the passenger seat, not that Eddie could hear him.

Back in his office, he let the girl have her fun. "Okay, Miss Martian. I'll bite," he said to her. "Where's your spaceship?"

"They abandoned us here," she said. Her tone was meek. Quiet. Reserved. Defeated, even. "We came here as researchers. Scouts to investigate the feasibility of future contact. It was our job to learn the culture, identify the dangers, probe for in-routes. There's not many of us. Maybe twenty left on the planet."

"I don't believe you," he said.

That was the only part of our conversation that felt like a lie.

But that was in his office. Out here on the highway, Sheriff Marty needed all his attention just to keep his car shiny side up. He thought of trying to hook her rear fender with his front bumper in a PIT maneuver to end the pursuit himself. The longer they stayed on the highway, the more likely they were for this to end with someone dead. But at these speeds, on these roads...

How long has it been since I've even done a PIT? Three, four years at least.

A poorly executed PIT could kill the suspect, kill him, kill any bystanders...

His radio hand mic sat in the passenger seat out of reach. He peeled his hand off the wheel and stretched for the cord coming out of the radio. His eyes bounced back and forth between the highway and the cord. With one hand skating the interceptor through the slush, he reeled the mic back in with his other hand. As soon as he had it, he keyed the push-to-talk button.

"Dispatch, Car One," he said.

"Go ahead, Car One." This was Jenny. Dispatch, clerk, payroll... she wore a lot of hats.

"Get a hold of Roseau. We're headed their way, northbound on Highway Four. Tell them we're coming in hot."

His mind flashed back to the questioning in his office that morning. She'd waived her right to representation and had been compliant ever since Eddie brought her in. Her I'm-an-alien story was unexpected. Unexpected, but detailed.

"There was a war. A planet-wide conflict. I suppose it would be considered a civil war from your vantage point," she told him. "I wasn't there for it. I was already here by the time it started. Although, looking back, we all should've seen it coming. It had been brewing for decades."

"So now comes the flying saucers and death rays," he said.

"No. All that was going on back home. As for us, well, the budget was 're-prioritized.' We didn't just 'beam' her. Believe it or not, it costs a lot of money to travel between the stars. With everything going towards the war-effort, the dream of peaceful contact between planets was all but forgotten. No way they were going to spend all that time and money to come get us when they were busy fighting a war. There was thirty of us when we first got here. Meanwhile, thousands were dying back home."

"So..." Sheriff Marty said. He could spend all day poking holes in her story, and he wanted to, if only for his own satisfaction. But her story really wasn't the point. Time to bring it back down to Earth. "So you took up stealing cars?"

She sighed. "We've all switched bodies a couple times now. I have no idea what my fellow scouts look like or where they're staying. We've lost contact with each other. We're all strangers in a strange land now. Alone. No contact from home. No mission. No purpose," she said. The way she said it, how solemn she spoke, none of it seemed like lies. "Can we... Can we talk somewhere more alone? Without all these other people around? Just you and me?"

Sheriff Marty peeked past her out his office door to the small town Sheriff Department bullpen. Eddie was out on the roads. Jenny was watering a plant on her desk. The water cooler gurgled. No way was Marty going to put himself into a compromising situation where it was just him and a vulnerable suspect by shutting his office door. Baseless acquisitions from criminals have ended careers. "I think we're private enough," he said.

Yet, here they were, alone, just him and her on a desolate highway roaring through jack pines, tamaracks and snow-covered bean fields. He was chasing her, fixated on catching her, bringing her back into the warm, eager to hear her stupid impossible stories and fill just apart of the void Hannah made when she took her life.

Why did she do that? Would did my daughter want to escape so bad she swallowed all those pills?

And why does this girl needs to escape me just as badly?

Sheriff Marty had been parked along these empty roads enough to know they were driving a wedge of chaos through the quiet as they drove. Ahead of the rattling, roaring Monte Carlo, crows were taking flight, and deer were flipping up their tails and leaping into the woods. Then silence would resume for a moment, only for the Interceptor to come along and kill the peace once again.

The landscape was silent before the Monte Carlo shattered it with its rattling muffler and V8 engine. Plumes of dust-like snow gushed up from the blacktop. Crows took flight. Deer took notice, flipped up their tails, and leapt back into the woods. Silence resumed for a moment, and then the Interceptor killed the peace once again.

When the Monte Carlo's brake lights lit up, Sheriff Marty caught up quick. He switched from gas to brake to match the girl. The back of the Ford listed to the left. Marty cranked the wheel just enough to put the squad car in a steady diagonal skid. The Monte Carlo took a sharp right turn off the county highway. Marty regained control in time to follow her, fishtailing as he made the turn.

As he steered and counter-steered, the girl put foot to gas pedal. The Monte Carlo kicked up rooster tails of slush and ice before the rubber found dry pavement and catapulted the car forward. She drove better than most, but not better than Marty.

He followed her move for move, turn for turn, and when they nosed onto the new road, Marty was on the accelerator faster.

"Dispatch, suspect is now westbound on… What fucking road are we even on?"

"Car One, this is Dispatch. Say again?"

"We're westbound on…" Marty said, craning his neck over the dash, trying to catch the words on the little green street signs they passed every half-mile. "Shit! She's turning again!"

Marty dropped the mic in favor of the wheel. It bounced and sprung back towards the radio on its spiral cord. He cranked on the wheel, passing it from hand to hand while pumping the brakes and bringing the Interceptor through a controlled slide. The squad car stopped its sideways motion only when he hammered the gas and the engine pulled it forward.

You're not getting away. Not if I have to chase you to the ends of the Earth.

That sounded like a hollow threat, even just in his head.

The Monte Carlo and the girl were on a new road now, narrower, more desolate, flanked on either side by frozen pastures with Stonehenge-like cattle that beared the cold because they had no other option. Marty didn't give the cows a passing glance. He paid no heed to the small battered "Minimum Maintenance Road" sign either. The road was more a crushed path through the snow than a plowed roadway. Ruts and potholes slowed the pace and jarred the drivers.

Where the hell is she leading me?

And then the brake lights of the Monte Carlo came on, solid and constant this time. The wheels of the Monte Carlo cut hard left and she sent the car skidding sideways to a stop, blocking the whole width of the farm road.

Sheriff Marty put two feet on the brake pedal. The ABS clattered the brakes on and off until finally the Interceptor came to a rest twenty feet from the sideways Monte Carlo. Marty clicked off his seatbelt and threw open his door. As he stepped out, he drew his sidearm and leveled it at the driver's door of the Monte Carlo.

Gotcha.

Her door opened. Her hands raised above the door as her foot stepped out. She exited the vehicle as meekly as she spoke. It was clear she didn't want to get shot. Wasn't looking for a suicide-by-cop escape route. That was good.

But what does she want?

"Keep your hands where I can see them," Sheriff Marty commanded even though she was already complying.

She stepped clear of the car door and kept her hands up in the air. Here was this shy young Sioux girl, underdressed in just jeans and a hoodie, looking short and thin even in the baggy sweatshirt, visibly shivering and scared.

Why? Why come all the way out here just to give up?

"Lay down on the ground," Sheriff Marty commanded. It seemed overly cautious and aggressive. But out here all by himself, without Dispatch or back-up having a clue where he was... He kept the gun trained on the girl.

"But it's cold," she said, looking down at the snow-packed farm road.

"Lay down, or I will put you down. Running like you did was a big mistake, missy. No more mister nice guy out here," Sheriff Marty said.

"I just wanted to be alone with you," she called back, her quiet voice barely bridging the twenty-foot gap of cold country wind between them. "This body won't last me much longer."

"Enough of the alien shit. It was cute back in the station, and as soon as we're back there, you can tell me all about your galactic war and flying saucers and missions from mars," Marty said. "Out here, you are going to lay down on this road so I can cuff you and bring you back. That's all that's happening out here. Got it?"

"No," she said.

That inky whirlpool flashed behind her eyelids. Her breathing pattern changed, became deeper and more deliberate.

"Don't try anything!" Sheriff Marty said. He flicked the safety off the sidearm. "I don't want this to end bad, but if you try something, I will fire."

"You should let me go," she said, not moving, not geographically anyway. Her hands stayed in the air. Her feet were planted. Still, something inside her churned.

"That's not going to happen. Will never happen," Marty said. "I don't want to shoot you but-"

"No one is out here but us. You can say you called off the pursuit. You should have done that miles back. These roads are dangerous. For both of us," she said.

She's not giving in. She's going to force me to do something. But maybe I don't have to shoot her. What is she? A buck ten soaking wet?

"Listen," Sheriff Marty called to her. "I'll make you a deal. I'll holster this gun if you promise me you won't resist. I'll even come to you. We'll put on some cuffs and have a nice safe ride back to the station. Deal?"

"Out here, out on this road, miles from town, you have to understand how I feel," she said, showing no sign she'd even heard his offer. "Our friends have no idea where we are. Your radio is out of range. My planet has abandoned me in favor of war and death. No one is coming to help either us."

"I'm putting my gun away, and I'm going to get out my handcuffs," Marty said.

"Don't!" she yelled.

It made him stop. His sidearm was halfway to his holster, his free hand he held up in the international hand sign of "Stop."

"Don't," she said. "Keep the gun aimed at me. Don't come any closer, or I'll have to do something."

Sheriff Marty frozen in that stance, empty hand up, palm facing this strange girl, sidearm aimed down at the road. His eyes squinted, as if that could help his brain uncover her intentions.

"What happens if I let you go? Then what? You go back to stealing cars and we do all this over again in a few days?" he asked.

"I'll go away. You'll never see me again," she said.

"What about your family? Your mom?"

"I'm not her daughter. Not really."

"I'm not buying this alien gag," Sheriff Marty said. But he couldn't pretend he didn't see that black flicker behind her eyes. The truth was, he wanted to know. Wanted to peel back her eyes and see what was really inside.

"You don't have to believe me, Sheriff. Just know that right now, we are both as alone as we've ever been. You have your friends back in town, but I'm used to being alone. This is nothing new to me. Even surrounded by humans, I'm alone. Leave me this way or become me. But if you really want to understand why she did it, well, just keep standing right there," she said.

"What— What do you mean 'why she did it'?" Marty demanded.

What did that mean? This is… This… Well, this is a joke. No way she could mean Hannah.

Sheriff Marty smirked.

She's just a kid, a scared and confused teenage girl. Not that different than a hundred other scared and confused girls from poor families in a poor community. She never knew Hannah. And she's not a damn alien. She's not even a threat. She just needs a friend.

He unfroze and holstered his gun. "Come on," he said and waved a hand for her to come to him. "I'm not going to shoot you. Hell, I won't even put the cuffs on. Just come over here and we'll get this all sorted out back in town. Back where it's warm."

He saw her shiver. Figured she was cold in that flimsy hoodie. Hell, he was cold. The damn cows in the fields were cold.

It wasn't a shiver from the cold. The next time she shook, she shivered right out of her skin. Something ink-black and comprised almost entirely of tentacles came out of her. It peeled her off like a kid discarding a snowsuit in a race for mom's hot chocolate. It was wet, glistening at first, and then growing frost as the wind hit its salamander-like skin. It wheeled towards Marty, its tentacles like spokes.

His brain was slow to believe his eyes. That fatherly smile he'd affected for the sake of the girl… maybe for the sake of himself… was slow to leave his face. His hand, still resting on the butt of his gun was even slower. The sidearm stayed holstered the entire time the creature burrowed inside of him. He was still smiling when it became him.

He looked across the frozen road to the limp and deflated body of the girl next to the Monte Carlo. He debated stepping over the corpse to leave in the Monte Carlo instead of the police car. It would be less conspicuous. Then again, the police car had advantages.

This old body won't last long. Best I get inside the cop car and pull over another kid. Then I can move on.

He turned from the girl and the Monte Carlo and walked back to the Interceptor. He climbed in and shut the door. When he heard the radio broadcast a staticed voice requesting updates, he grabbed the spiral cable and ripped it out of the plug-in. He threw the mic back to the passenger seat and put the car in reverse.

All alone now. Everyday a struggle to survive. Everyday a lie. Finally, he understood.

Monster Mike Goes to the Dentist

"Can I pay in cash? I don't really have insurance," Monster Mike told the receptionist.

"We can set up a payment plan if you'd like," she smiled.

Monster Mike smiled back and told himself not to eat her. All he had to do was play it cool, let the humans pull his aching tooth, and walk away. He pulled a couple hundreds out of his pants pocket. He smoothed them flat and made sure she saw old Benjamin's smirking face of the fronts of the bills. He hoped she didn't notice the moisture.

"Mike?" a woman called from a hallway around the side of the desk.

Mike stuffed the cash back in his pocket. He looked to this new woman, clean and healthy and chipper and wearing scrubs, and then back to the cold and scrawny receptionist with her polite but uncomfortable smile.

"We can figure out the billing when you're finished," the receptionist said.

Leave me alone. Please, her eyes told Mike. Just go. She sort of nodded towards the new woman. Mike looked at the new woman, the dental hygienist he supposed, and saw that she was still legitimately happy and bright. He decided to go with her.

The two walked down a winding hall. Little rooms were on either side. Some had empty chairs. One had a chair with a kid in it. The next room had a big radiation gun dangling from the ceiling. Mike wiped the sweat from his brow.

The hygienist brought him to a room with an empty chair in the center. A radiation gun was mounted on the ceiling, but folded off to the side. A tray of little metal tools sat on an appendage growing off of the chair. A computer screen hung just above it. The back wall was a plate glass window looking out to the parking lot.

"Go ahead and have a seat, Mike," the hygienist said. "My name is Jill, and I'm going to do your cleaning today."

Mike sat. He eyed the radiation gun and then the tray of tools next to the chair. He decided he could deal with the tools. The gun... "You said cleaning. You don't use that gun for cleanings, do you?"

"Well, since this is your first time here we'd like to get a pano or at least some bite wings if we could," Jill said as she sat in a little stool, arranging the tools on the tray.

"I... I don't think my insurance covers that," Mike said. Did Jill hear his conversation with the other one at the front desk? Did she see the wet hundreds?

"Oh. Well, most policies do cover x-rays. Are you sure-"

"No x-rays. I have... I have a heart condition. The ticker. The ticker just can't take it," Mike lied.

Jill sat back, stationary for one minute. "Huh. Well, okay then."

She bought it. That was good. He was going to get through this. Just so long as he could hold it together for this one interaction. "Yeah. Damndest thing. Insurance. What a crock, right?" he went on. That was good. That was something a human would say, right?

"Yeah," Jill drew out the word.

Maybe that last part was too much. Maybe he should lay off the act.

"Well, I'm going to lean you back here and take a look around," she said and pushed some button or lever. The back of Mike's chair began to descend. It took him by surprise and instead of lying down with the chair, he sat up.

"No need to look around too much, really. It's just the one tooth, see?" he said and pulled down the right side of his lips. "Chipped it and ever since then it's been killing me. Don't know if you got a vise-grips around here or maybe a..."

Jill laughed.

Mike scowled. Was she mocking him?

"Come on," she said. "Really now. I have to look inside your mouth if we're going to get anything done. Just lay back and let me have a peak. I'll be gentle. Promise."

This Jill, the way she smiled, the way she laughed, the way she said "Promise"... Maybe she wasn't taunting him. Mike had to test her out. Had to know if she'd betray him.

"You know, those tools there," he said, pointing to the tray. "Don't you think that's kind of cliché?"

"Cliché? What are you talking about?"

"Well, you know. Like every torture chamber with a chair in it has some tray full of weird twisted metal tools on it. I mean, it's kind of been done, you know? You have to know what I'm talking about, right?"

Jill laughed again. "You are a riot! Torture chambers... This is a dentist's office!" she said. "'Sides, it's kind of hard for me to clean your teeth without any tools, silly."

"So, no torture?" Mike said.

"No torture."

"I can handle some torture. I just wasn't expecting it. Are you sure you don't have a vise-grips or maybe a needle nosed-"

"No torture!" Jill said. "And no, I'm not going to start ripping teeth out of your skull with a needle nosed pliers. Come on now, you big goof. Lay down and let me have a look."

"Okay. Fine. But no matter what you see, let's just keep this professional, okay?" Mike said.

"Oh," Jill said, not laughing now. "Sure. Absolutely."

Mike laid down in the chair. Jill pulled a little paper mask over her mouth and nose. She picked up two of the torture instruments off the tray.

"Now open up and say 'Ahh'."

Mike laid down and opened his maw. He knew enough about humans to know she didn't actually want him to say 'Ahh' but just open his mouth. Jill seemed satisfied and leaned in. She put the little mirror tool inside his lips and began prodding around with her poking tool.

"So, any big plans for the summer?" she asked him.

This had to be a test. She was checking to see if he'd use his second mouth to respond. That was the only explanation for her questioning him while she had the instruments in his mouth. Wiser than the average monster, Mike waited.

"No. Nothing big. A few clean-up projects is about all," he said after the tools were out of his mouth. Then he unhinged his jaw again so she could continue to poke around.

"Don't I know it. I have so many chores to do around the yard I swear I'll be busy till Labor..." She stopped. "What's this back here?"

Mike clamped down, tools be damned. Jill recoiled.

"Sorry," Mike said. The bent tools fell from his mouth when he spoke.

"No. It's my fault. I must have poked your gums too hard," Jill said and went about picking the instruments off the floor. "Are you okay?"

"Yeah. Fine. No problem. Just... I mean. We're keeping this professional, right? I just need this one tooth pulled. This one right here," he pointed. "It's killing me."

"Yeah. Of course. Professional," Jill said. "Let me just grab some clean tools."

Mike watched her. She took up a new poker instrument and another mirror instrument. She readied herself and then leaned back in. Mike opened wide.

"It's this tooth?" she asked.

"Uh huh," Mike grunted.

"No other problems? Nothing else is bothering you?"

"Uh uh," Mike said.

"Nothing back by your molars? Back here?" Jill said, leaning in closer to his incisors. She maneuvered the poker past his canines, past his molars, back towards the sphincter of his throat and the razor sharp rings of tiny teeth surrounding it. She poked at one of the hundreds of concentric teeth. "Back here?"

That was it. The jig was up. She knew. Mike took a moment to breathe, and then did what he knew he needed to do.

Mike unhinged his jaw, really unhinged it this time. He flexed open the aperture of his gullet and wrapped the hundreds of tiny razor teeth around both of Jill's wrists. Then he clinched and separated her hands from her body.

Screaming, she pulled loose the two stumps. Blood pumped out of her arteries like sporadic little red fountains. The way she waved them around, she sprayed the rooms with dotted red lines. When she ran out of breath, she took in a quick deep chest-full of air and then kept screaming.

Mike spat out the two metal tools. Those things would hurt coming out. Then he turned towards Jill as she continued to cry. "The Thing is, Jill, I thought we were keeping this professional."

She wasn't shutting up. Others would come running soon. There was only one thing to do. Mike climbed up out of the chair and showed his true nature. Sometimes it felt good to let go. If he had his way, he'd be like this all the time. He had to enjoy these rare moments when they came along.

Mike stood over Jill and his head became all mouth. Teeth and maw and saliva and tongues. He wrapped his mouth over Jill's head and shoulders. Her screams became muffled. His lamprey-like teeth chewed and sawed and separated flesh and bones. Mike swallowed like a man dying of thirst drank water. Jill went silent. When enough flesh and ligaments were cut, her lower body flopped to the tile floor.

The receptionist rushed into the room. That judgmental heaving hawk. Mike roared at her and watched her turn pale and woozy. He thought about chewing her head off too, but digestion was hard work, and more humans would quickly follow.

Mike turned toward the big picture window on the far side of the room. He took two strides and jumped through the glass. It shattered into a million pieces. He landed outside in the parking lot on all four feet. Mike galloped towards his car and away from the dentist office.

God damn his tooth still hurt.

#

There was a Starbucks down the road. If he couldn't use his cash for a tooth extraction, maybe he could use it to ease the pain with some coffee. Humans seemed to enjoy the beverage. It smelled good. The heat of it must be good to sooth an aching tooth. All it would take was a few minutes of acting normal. He checked himself in the rearview mirror to make sure he looked human again.

Yep, just a normal guy in a normal car. Just a fella who wanted some coffee who had nothing to do with all the lights and sirens headed in the opposite direction. He was sure a coffee would calm his nerves. A coffee would set him straight again.

Monster Mike pulled up to the little menu board and speaker box.

"Welcome to Starbucks, my name is Karen. What can I get you today?" the speaker box said.

"Medium coffee," Mike said. He'd heard humans order coffee before. He was going to nail this. "Black. No cream. No sugar."

"Okay. You mean a Venti Americano?"

Mike ground his hundreds of teeth and embraced the pain radiating from the one. He rubbed his eyes and reminded himself to stay the part for just this one short transaction. "Can you do me a favor, Karen? Can we just keep this professional?"

Pizza Face

Snoots, the Maine Coon pride-queen, had never seen the pride this bad off. They'd suffered before. Gone without food before, without fresh water or litter before. Were abandoned by God for days, even weeks at a time. But God always returned. Always. Now…

The blistered and bloated face of God smelled of rot. It leaked pus through His pores, and blood from lesions. Snoots crept up God's chest, put her nose close to God's and sniffed, not wanting to believe what she knew was true. Unable to tolerate so much evidence to the contrary, that the worst of all calamities had beset them, she turned away from the face of God. Still, she provided God with the customary rub to express her and all the pride's subordinance to Him, finishing with her tail close to his face. But Snoots couldn't help herself. She circled back to the God's face for one more sniff, then quickly turned again to run her torso against Him and present Him her behind with tail raised, as was tradition. God was unresponsive.

Snoots prodded the jelly-like chest of God before sitting down to survey the house.

At fourteen years of age, the long-haired gray Maine Coon was old enough to remember better times. Times when a new cat being introduced to the pride was a holy blessing, rather than a strain on resources. Times before the Gods drank. Before the Gods were unemployed. Before the Gods became divorced and the woman-God left them with the man-God. In those ancient days, they always had fresh water and proper food. The pets came more often and with more enthusiasm. Snoots remembered when the Gods brought them special food They called "treats" and a mesmerizing herb They called "catnip." Those days seemed like a dream now.

She remembered the Gods eating better too. Lavish, sacramental meals at the forbidden table of macaroni and cheese, spaghetti, steak, and barbeque chicken. After the divorce, when just the man-God remained, it was nearly all pizza. Maybe the occasional box of Chinese delivery. Then the man-God died.

For weeks now, the pride had survived off scraps from the pizza boxes scattered through the house. So many pizza boxes. The only item more prevalent in the house was the beer cans. And the feces. Snoots had decreed the beer unsafe to drink, as the members of the pride who didn't believe her quickly found out for themselves. The same went for the tobacco spit inside the beer cans with the ripped open top. The pizza, however, was their last lifeline.

As queen, Snoots had insisted the rest of the pride eat before she did. When she finally allowed herself to eat, there was nothing left in last pizza box but a few strands of dried-hard cheese and grease soaked into the cardboard. She'd ordered the others to leave the room while she ate, if she could call it eating. Then she proceeded to lick dry the grease spots at the bottom of the box. Oh heavens! how she licked for what seemed like hours. Each dry pass with her tongue brought her little more than the memories of flavor but she kept at it anyway. If all she managed was to trick her brain into thinking she was eating, even if nothing reached her belly, so be it. She'd lay on the box and lick the darkened cardboard for an eternity just to fool herself into thinking the pain in her stomach was going to go away.

It never did.

The scouts would find more, Snoots told herself. There were so many pizza boxes, hidden in so many places across the house. From the heights of the kitchen counter to the depths below furniture. Buried in the piles of garbage. Under dirty laundry. The bedroom. There were so many boxes in the bedroom where the man-God had slept before dying. Perhaps under the bed or under the covers, the scouts would find another box with whole slices remaining. There was always another place to look Even after His death, God would provide.

Snoots looked around the house, perched on top of the dead God's chest, who had died reclined in His chair. The elevation wasn't as high as the forbidden kitchen counter, but Snoots doubted she could make the jump up to the counter anyway. She'd become so weak. Her perch from on top of God on top of the recliner would have to do.

Even so, the view from there was a sight she wished she didn't have to see. What was once a safe and happy home was now a wasteland. Feces dirty clothes, beer cans, and empty pizza boxes from wall to wall. Inedible molds on those walls. The corpse of Nibbles in the hallway, the first and still unburied of the pride to fall. More would die soon, unless Snoots could find a solution.

And there was the smell. Urine mostly. With the litter box as overloaded as it was, the pride had taken to relieving themselves wherever they stood. The more mature tried to find suitable places, like the dead houseplant or in the more absorbent piles of garbage and dirty clothes, but nothing hid the smell. The stench was unbearable. Truly, they were living beyond the day of Armageddon.

But Snoots had decreed, and they had obeyed, that no cat was to defecate near God. If they lost everything else, at least they could maintain their own nobility. Their majesty was passed down to them by the Gods. To desecrate a God was to desecrate the entire pride.

Her memory flashed to the grease stains on the empty pizza box. Had she displayed the stoic nobility demanded by her position when she sat for hours licking at the stain? As queen of the pride, had she acted with honor when she cast them out so she could grovel at the feet of her own mocking starvation? Was that how a queen, the pride's pathway to God Himself, should behave?

No one saw her that day. When she'd had her moment of weakness, she made sure no one else was around.

"Queen Snoots!" a call came out. Winky, her most loyal servant came weaving along the path through the garbage from the hallway to the recliner. "Bad news, m'lady."

"There is nothing good or bad, but thinking makes it so," Snoots said. "Come up here, my sister, so we may speak face to face."

The Tabby came to the recliner and leaped up to the armrest. Winky had been given her name by God due to the colors of her eyes. The right half of her face was black and the left was orange. The pigment of her eyes was opposed to the colors of her coat. Her right eye was a bright green surrounded by the field of black fur. Her left eye was solid blue.

"Now, what is the bad news you speak of?" Snoots asked those two mismatched eyes.

"The scouts have returned, m'lady. As you commanded me, I ordered them to every corner of the house in search of more pizza. More food of any kind," Winky said.

"And what did they report?" Snoots asked.

"There's no more food, m'lady. None. We've searched every inch of the house to exhaustion. There's no more pizza boxes to pry open. No more garbage cans to rummage through. No more food in the cupboard we can open. The metal cans… we know there's food inside. We can see the pictures on the cans taunting us with their contents but…"

"It's okay, my sister," Snoots said. She reached out and put her paw on top of Winky's, calming her if only for the moment. "Are you certain there are no more pizza boxes to be found and opened?"

"None, m'lady. I'm afraid we're out of options," Winky said. "No options but—"

"Don't. Not you," Snoots said firmly. "I'll not hear of it. Not from the least of the pride but especially from you, my good and faithful servant. If we do not maintain our honor, we have nothing. Now more than ever. Especially now that we know the food is gone."

"But what will we do, m'lady?"

"The Gods will provide," Snoots said. "They always have. We keep our honor, we keep our faith, and the Gods will rescue us. If your empty stomach causes you pain, fill it with faith in the Gods and They will ease your suffering."

"Yes, my queen, but—"

"Winky, I trust you more than all the rest of the pride. They hold you in high esteem, nearly as high as they hold me, their queen. Do you understand what I'm telling you? When I go, and it won't be long now, you will reign over the pride. The burden will fall on your shoulders, and you must keep up their spirits. You must maintain our nobility."

"I understand, m'lady."

"Now," Snoots said, sticking out her chest. "What of the wood chute? Our efforts there must now be our priority."

"Our only hope, m'lady," Winky said. "I've put our youngest and healthiest on the task of climbing the chute and reaching the door. The chute itself is smooth metal and steep. Too steep. Poofball nearly reached the top this morning but had nothing but his momentum to drive him up to the door. When his momentum ran out, he tried to dig in with his claws, but the metal... it was no use. What's more, I'm afraid even if one of them is able to reach the top and get to the door, it will be latched and sealed shut. Our salvation as close and as far away as the food inside of those cans."

Snoots nodded slowly. "The safety of the pride comes first. We can't have another incident like the dryer vent."

"Mister Whiskers never returned from that expedition. And now his corpse clogs what might have been our only viable escape route," Winky said.

"Please, Winky. Don't speak so harshly of our fallen. Others may hear," Snoots said.

"Yes, m'lady," Winky said. He seemed to take a moment to look over the house from Snoots' perch. A disaster. A throne no one could ever want. A burden no cat would ask to bear. "What are your orders, m'lady?"

"Go to the basement to the wood chute. I'm too weak to travel these days. I'll need you to make a decision for me. If the chute is truly unclimbable, if the door leading outside looks latched and offers no hope, call off the efforts. We'll find another way out," Snoots said.

"Right away, m'lady," Winky said and leapt down from the recliner.

For a moment, Snoots was alone with the dead God. She contemplated their fate, and with each passing moment, she found their prospects bleaker. No more food. No escape. The long-held values and traditions of the pride were fraying at the seams. She turned back to the face of God, a vestige once so happy and lively, now wet with stinking yellow fluid seeping out of the skin and red boils dotting the nose, cheeks, and forehead.

It wasn't her place to question the Gods, but the words spilled out of her empty core unprovoked. "Why, God? Why have you forsaken us to the fate?" Snoots wherpered.

"M'lady?" another call came up to the recliner.

Snoots whipped around, hoping her new visitor hadn't heard her speak in such ways to God.

A rail-thin Shorthair sat at the foot of the recliner. One of the younger cats who had only come to the pride after the divorce. These young ones who had never seen the good days, their faith was the most fragile. His tail swished back and forth across an empty pizza box.

"Flufflebutt, my child," Snoots greeted the shorthair by name. She knew each by name, by the names given to them by the Gods.

"M'lady, I'm hungry," Flufflebutt said.

"I know, my child. We all are. Keep your heart filled with faith and the Gods will provide food for your body," Snoots said.

"But God is dead, my queen," Flufflebutt said.

"There are others," Snoots said. "We must maintain our nobility until another God arrives to provide for us."

"M'lady, this God may yet provide," Flufflebutt said.

The conversation had been heard by a few others nearby. His last blasphemy perked their ears and drew their attention. Mittens leapt down from the counter and made her way through the trash. Snuffles peaked out from under a pile of trash. Even Winky came back, too early from her mission to the wood chute. The Ragamuffin scouts, Stinky and Inky flanked her.

The brazen kitten, if he had come to Snoots privately perhaps she could have educated the youth. But his public display left her little options. "My child, do not sit there and suggest such things before your queen and God Himself," Snoots said loud and clear so all could hear.

"This God is dead," Flufflebutt said. "In life, He always cared for us. Perhaps in death—"

"Hold your sinful tongue, Flufflebutt," Snoots commanded. "Before it spills out something you'll regret."

"M'lady, we've all been thinking it. We smell God every day, stronger than any garbage, any remains of pizza, even the urine. It taunts us! The God could save us yet if we—"

"Silence!" Snoots cried louder than she'd managed in days. "We have honor in the pride, even if you've forgotten it! We are a noble family and we will act as the Gods would have demanded of us."

"What about Mittens who just came from the forbidden counter?" Flufflebutt said. "You yourself, oh queen, have commanded us to search through the garbage. Would the Gods not condemn us for these transgressions? Haven't we already fallen from grace? Yet you keep from us the one sin He never forbid. The one sin that might save us. Save us all. Wouldn't God want—"

"How dare you suppose the will of God!" Snoots bellowed with all her remaining strength. And it was at that time, she knew what she must do. She didn't want to carry out the sentence, but Flufflebutt had left her no option. She would have avoided it if possible. But the pride needed a leader. They needed someone to carry out God's will as it truly was. Snoots knew what she must do.

"Flufflebutt, son of Minx, the third of her litter, with the authority bequeathed to me by God Himself, I pronounce thee A Bad Kitty," Snoots said.

Cries and whines rose up across the pride. They protested. Screeched. Flufflebutt, the brash kitten, was shocked. The expression on his face pained Snoots, but the kitten had brought it upon himself. Ashamed, Flufflebutt ran. As he fled from

157

the pride, others hissed at him. The pair of Ragamuffin scouts swatted at him as he ran.

Good. Let Flufflebutt run and hide. And if the pride ostracizes him, all the better. Better to lose one cat than the honor of the entire pride.

Winky leapt back up to the armrest. She stepped onto the God's belly and stood close to Snoots.

"You've gone too far, my queen," she said quietly, too quietly for the rest to hear. "You know I respect your reign and envy your wisdom, but Flufflebutt—"

"Flufflebutt brought his sentence upon himself," Snoots said.

"You labeled him a curse only a God could give. Never in catkind have we ever uttered those words to one another," Winky said. "You are our true and noble queen, but you are no God."

"Don't you understand, Winky? Our only hope now is in the favor of the Gods. If we keep the faith, another will come and we'll be saved. But if we throw away Their grace with blasphemy, we are all truly lost," Snoots said. "In the meantime, in the absence of God, one of us must rise up."

"No cat is equal to a God," Winky said.

"These are dark times, my sister," Snoots said. "This reign, it is a curse I'm all too eager to surrender. And remember, one day you will take this heavy mantle from me, and you will have to make such rulings. Do you think I enjoyed saying those words? They were poison to my very lips."

"But they came out all the same," Winky said.

"Aye. And only if I had some true poison to end the torture," Snoots said.

"Don't say such things, my queen," Winky said. "We need your leadership. We need you to keep the pride together. I don't mean disrespect but... A Bad Ki—"

"Don't. Don't spoil your lips the way I have mine," Snoots said. "But so help me, I will not hear of what Flufflebutt proposed. Not from any of us. And so help me, if I ever wither so weak as to suggest that course of action myself, kill me, my sister."

"M'lady—" Winky said, taken back.

"I have given my commands. Return to your mission at the wood chute. If we are to escape this hell without divine intervention, it is through that chute."

"Yes, m'lady." And off she went, coursing along the paths they'd made through the wasteland the house had become, to the stairs and back down to the basement.

The others had gone back to their distractions as well. Some slept. Others foraged. Stinky and Inky had enough energy to cry at each other and exchange a few swats, arguing about the ruling Snoots had handed down. They didn't have to like her rulings, but they'd obey all the same.

Snoots let out a long echoing cry. "Why?" she asked no one and expected no response. He turned to the face of the God and asked again, quieter the time. "Why?"

Why did life lead them all here to this desperate and hollow place? Why did the God surrender to Death so long before another came to replace Him? How was it that a God could die at all?

Snoots laid down, her eyes wet with emotion and fear. What would become of them? Would another God ever show up to deliver them? What had they done to deserve this? How had Snoots, as the pride-queen failed the Gods to earn them the hell?

Nothing. She'd done nothing to deserve this. She'd led the pride for years of loyal worship of the Gods. She'd kept their nobility. Demanded their honor. Had she not swatted those whom the Gods shooed off the counters? Who'd piddled on the carpet? Who drank from half-full glasses of milk? She had. And the Gods had exalted her to her position as pride-queen. And now...

The Gods had abandoned them. First the woman-God and now the man-God. Still, Snoots fought to maintain Their God-hood. After all these years, was she supposed to abandon the faith now? Never! Never would she let the pride dishonor Them by... by... Snoots couldn't say it. Couldn't think it! But even for her, the temptation was there.

Shortly after God died, He'd left a nearly whole pie on the counter. The box wide open and just one slice removed. It was a beautiful meal. A banquet large enough for the whole pride. The yellow of the cheese. The bulbous raised bread of the crust.

The sweet and savory pools of butter. The rich and satisfying bits of sausage. Oh, how they had feasted as soon as Snoots allowed them onto the counter.

She could still smell the scent of the pizza on the God. Especially on His fingers.

Those fingers, once so ready to grant pets and scratches, now limp and swelled and lifeless.

But still smelling of pizza.

Snoots dug her nose into the fingers, telling herself she was just wishing for pets and scratches, hoping beyond hope that they'd regain their strength and itch behind her ears. Oh God, how good it would feel! How reassuring to have a power and authority higher than her own to keep the pride in line! How comforting to feel the rise and fall of the God's chest breathe in and out! How just the world had been.

But the fingers still smelled of pizza, and God how hungry Snoots had become!

She thought of the stain in the pizza box she'd spent hours licking, ashamed and humiliated but addicted all the same.

Snoots looked down from her perch. The others had wandered off, either to sleep and conserve energy or to use what little strength they had to find food or escape. Snoots looked back to the God's fingers.

She salivated. Her tongue lashed out and brushed aside her whiskers. One lick. One lick might give her just enough nutrition to survive another day and maintain her reign over the pride. She couldn't trust Winky. Not after today. She had sinister thoughts stirring inside her cat mind. One lick. Hadn't Snoots licked the Gods fingers before, when they were alive and ready to grant pets? Then why not in death?

A drop of saliva fell from her chin. His nose so close to the fingers, when her tongue went out to scoop up the saliva, it brushed God-skin.

It tasted like pizza.

The next lick came without thinking, but not by accident. And the next. She couldn't stop herself now. She was ravaging over the leftover oils and flavors left by the pizza on the hand of God. It wasn't so sinful. She'd licked God's hand before.

Why was this any different?

When her teeth sank into flesh, the skin ruptured like the thinnest membrane. Snoots tasted blood and felt no compulsion to stop.

"Queen Snoots!"

Snoot sat up and looked down from the recliner. They were back. Winky at the center of them. God's hand was down below the armrest. Snoots had been hidden from their view when her teeth had broke skin. They saw nothing.

"Winky, my sister. Snuffles. Stinky. Inky. Mittens…" Snoot greeted them. Then she saw Flufflebutt and her disposition changed. "Bad Kitty, you dare to approach me so soon?"

"I'm not alone, my queen," Bad Kitty said.

Snoots turned to her right-hand cat, her sister, and closest confidant. "Winky, what's the meaning of this rabble?"

"The wood chute is unclimbable. Its door impenetrable. The food is gone. You've uttered words of the Gods. Is there a better time for us to meet and form a congress?" Winky said.

"A congress?" Snoots asked. "Are we a pack of dogs that we lead by a congress? You forget our honor, my sister."

"And you've gone too far, my queen. You are not our God with the authority to pass down such holy condemnation to Flufflebutt," Winky said.

"He has another name now," Snoots said. "Take heed or earn yourself a similar name."

"You're no God. You've overstepped your bounds," Winky said.

"Our God is dead, and until another sees fit to come and save us from this hell, I'll reign here."

"There's names for Gods who reign in hell," Bad Kitty said.

Snoots raised up, arched her back, and hissed. "Do you see amongst yourselves something better?"

"Perhaps," Winky said. "Perhaps I see in myself a queen who can feed her pride."

"You too, then!" Snoots hissed.

The Maine Coon was larger than the rest of the pride, even though her core was emaciated with starvation. Her fur was thick and long. Every hair stuck out wide and daunting. Her pupils widened to the size of dimes.

Winky rose up her hairs too. A mohawk along the Tabby's spine. She strutted around the recliner, wide measured steps. Any moment ready to pounce.

"It doesn't have to be this way, my queen. Let us have Him," Winky said.

"Over my dead body," Snoots said.

"Over His," Winky said and pounced.

Snoots jumped to meet her. They crashed together near the God's midsection, Winky with more weight and momentum than Snoots. They landed, Winky on top of Snoots on top of God's stomach. That was fine. That let Snoots fight with all four paws. Winky had been too impetuous and headstrong to measure her attack. She'd suffer for it, and then she would be A Bad Kitty too!

But Winky fought with a fury Snoots didn't expect, and didn't have the strength to repulse. One paw, spread wide and tipped with razor sharp claws caught Snoots across the nose. Her hiss melted into a cry and she rolled off the recliner and onto a mound of beer cans. Before she could twist back to her feet, Winky was on him again, sinking needles through her bottlebrush coat and into her back. Snoots cried out again, feeling more than just the pain. Feeling the betrayal. The shame. The fall from grace. All of their fall from grace. They had nothing now.

Winky dealt one more claw swat, and Snoots set off running through the garbage and debris. Her loyal scouts, Stinky and Inky hissed and took swipes at her as she ran, just as they had to Bad Kitty.

Snoots didn't run far, just into the shadows down the hallway. Close enough to see and hear what happened next. Not far from Nibble's corpse. Snoots' failure began here and was now complete here.

Winky limped back to the foot of the recliner. With a double wind-up, she leapt back on top of the recliner and on top of the dead God. She took a moment to lick her wounds. She hadn't gotten out of the fight clean, at least Snoots could say that much. But the way Winky took her time. The way the rest of the pride looked to her patiently, respectfully...

When Winky finished licking her hairs back in place, she sat up and looked over the pride.

"Flufflebutt," Winky called. "Come up here, my child."

Bad Kitty wove through the trash to the recliner and then joined Winky on top of the God.

"You didn't deserve the judgement passed down to you. You have been the bravest of all of us," Winky said. "Eat, my child."

Snoots whined from her spot down the hallway. "Noooooooooo."

"All hail Winky!" Mittens cried out from the pride surrounding the recliner. "Our new queen! Hail, Queen Winky!"

The others chimed in. Poofball. Snuffles. Stinky and Inky. Flufflebutt. They all hailed Winky as their new pride-queen.

And Winky nudged Flufflebutt closer to God. "Go ahead, my child. Eat. Don't be afraid. Start with the face. See? Doesn't it look just like a pizza?"

Nothing Inside

Jen saw the dead body and she didn't look away. The whitetail deer lay in tall yellowing grass. At first, it was nothing more than a brown hump, like a gopher mound. But as she walked closer, she saw it was a mature buck with a full eight point rack. It had been hit by at least a half dozen shots. Its blood had turned black. Its one visible eye was sunk into its skull.

"Sam, look," Jen said. "Somebody shot it, like a lot."

Her boyfriend, Sam came over. "Fucking shame. It's been dead for days. Look how swollen the belly is. They didn't even take the antlers. What a waste."

"Gross," she said. She didn't know what it was about the deer that made her linger over it, despite the smell and the little black bugs that were crawling over its eyes, nose, and mouth. If a part of her brain was taking in the site to apply it to some problem she hadn't yet resolved, all the mental work stayed in her subconscious.

Sam and Jen were dressed to bird hunt. She wore her father's old Carhart, the pockets filled with as many beer bottle caps and cigarette butts as shotgun shells. Sam had a vest with tubes for the shells and wore camouflage underneath the vest. They hadn't planned on seeing deer, alive or dead. Maybe a few turkeys, but it was weeks before the rut.

"Who would shoot a buck like that and then just leave it here?" she asked.

"A fucking asshole, that's who," Sam said. "Come on, let's keep going. I want to flush this clearing out."

Jen took another look at the bloated brown corpse, her alligator mind still trying to solve some riddle. It started to bubble up closer to the surface. Violence for the sake of violence. The bottle caps rattling around in her pocket. A pain she wasn't ready to admit existed.

"Come on, babe," Sam said to her. He wasn't kind to her by habit, but had a sense her mind had left the clear and gone to a less pleasant place. "Hey. Nevermind that thing."

"Yeah. Okay," she said.

He smiled at her. "You better get used to seeing that if you want to be a big tough Marine after we graduate."

Jen smiled. "Don't make fun of me. I could be a Marine if I wanted."

Sam laughed as he started walking through the clearing in the deep woods, his gun at the ready, waiting for a grouse to take flight. "You wouldn't make it through the first day of boot camp."

"Could make it longer than you," she said as she left the deer behind and hustled to stay abreast with Sam.

#

The grouse took flight like a bat out of hell. Its wings sounded like a straight-piped V8.

She had time for her heart to skip a beat, for her to raise up the shotgun barrel, for her to put a bead on it, click off the safety, and fire a shot. The gun blast ripped through the forest. A dozen song birds took flight. The grouse tumbled and crashed somewhere in the brush.

"Ha!" Jen stated, more than laughed.

"Lucky shot," Sam said and smiled.

The two trampled through the tall grass to where the bird went down.

"I need a good hunting dog. A dog would make this so much easier," Sam said.

"Found it," Jen said. She set her shotgun down and picked up the bird. It was smaller than a chicken. Its feathers were colored like the forest, beads of blood like the falling birch leaves around them. Jen broke its neck so it would die already. She handed it to Sam to bag and then collected her shotgun.

A gust of wind came and had just enough of a bite to remind her that colder days were ahead. The yellow grass swayed. A few of those reddened birch leaves fluttered to the ground. In the quiet of the woods, Jen found an overwhelming sense of being watched. Somewhere a coyote yipped and howled, or maybe it was a wolf.

"Ready to keep going?" Sam said.

"What the hell is that?" Jen asked.

"What the hell is what?"

She pointed. "That. Over by the tree line. We walked right by it."

Sam looked. "Is that… I think that might be a…"

#

The door to the bunker was dug into an earthen barrow like the cellar doors to an old farmhouse. The mound had a few vent pipes poking out from the top, but otherwise the bunker was perfectly hidden from the middle of the clearing. As they stood at the door, Jen could see the brown lump of the deer's body less than a hundred yards away.

Sam knelt down to examine the padlock. "It's unlocked," he said and slipped the bolt off the loop. "Looks like maybe they meant to lock it, but it didn't catch."

He turned the handle and stopped there.

"Should we?" Jen said.

"Are you crazy? What if someone is inside?" Sam said.

She looked around the clearing. "I don't see a truck or a four wheeler anywhere. We're the only two people dumb enough to walk this deep into the woods. Besides, there's no way we can just walk away now."

Sam smiled. The door latch was already open. All he had to do was pull up. The cellar door was made of thick steel and screeched as he pulled it open. The afternoon sun shined on the first few concrete steps leading down. After that, all was black.

"After you, Marine," he said.

"Whatever. I'm sure there's nothing inside." Still, she gripped her 12 gauge and went down the steps.

Dust motes drifted in the sunlight. The solid concrete walls seemed to absorb the rest of the light. As soon as her head was through the cellar door, she had to move deeper down the stairs by feel. The air was cool but musty. A sense that something was just inches from her face had joined the conviction that they were being watched. Carrying the shotgun one handed, she kept her other hand on the wall in hopes of finding a lightswitch.

"Are you coming or what?" she asked.

"Yeah. Hang on."

His boots shuffled against the concrete steps. The hinges on the rusted door whined. Then the door clanged shut with her and Sam inside. There was no light.

"Sam, you ass! I can't see shit!"

"It's fine. Just keep moving. There's got to be a light down here somewhere."

Almost on cue, her fingers found a switch and her feet found the bottom of the steps. Her fingers fumbled for a moment. She fought off her nerves and flipped it up.

Over head lights popped on, exposing the interior of the bunker.

There was a full kitchen with a small dinette table on one side, a living room with couches and a big TV on the other. The floor was tiled in the kitchen and covered in thick cushioned carpet in the living room. There was decorations and personal effects like a magazine on the coffee table and a deck of playing cards on the small dinette table. There were nature paintings on the walls and Mickey and Minnie salt and pepper shakers on the stove. Despite the place looked like it had been furnished during the 1980s, everything was clean and in it's place. Everything was carefully positioned to look like a normal happy, healthy, above ground house.

"Oh my god, Sam. Look at this place," Jen said.

"This looks like a photo come to life from my childhood," Sam said.

"No. It's way too perfect. Where are the holes punched in the walls and the cigarette burns in the armrests?"

"You're right. No blood on the walls or vomit on the carpet. I didn't even see an eviction notice on the front door."

Sam and Jen laughed.

"Oh my god. Sam, we could live down here," Jen said.

Sam laughed, not because he thought it was funny, but because she was right. The two went about exploring the rooms like Goldilocks in the house of the Three Bears. Sam exploring the kitchen first. Jen went into the living room.

"There's food in the cupboards. Mac and cheese, canned chili and vegetables, spaghetti, flour, sugar... This place is stocked!"

"Sam, you should see this DVD collection! It's like every movie ever made!" Jen said. "Whoa! There's an old Nintendo with a ton of games! Mario... Zelda... Excitebike... Paperboy! Oh my god, I love that game!"

"Jen!"

"What?"

"There's beer in the fridge. Like A LOT of beer! Like the whole fridge is beer!"

She abandoned her place, kneeling on the soft carpet in front of the entertainment center and went to Sam standing in front of the open fridge.

"Holy shit, that's a lot of Keystone Light."

"Jen, we could live here!"

It was a dumb idea; she knew it, but was too alluring to dismiss it. "Like a real husband and wife. Not like all the shitty versions up there. Like an actual honest-to-god in-love husband and wife."

"Oh yeah?"

She nodded. "We should find the bedroom."

#

Sam's face was slender and potted with spurts of hair growth. He was rude and swore and wasn't always kind, but how he handled Jen in the bedroom made up for all of that. He was strong, but never hurtful. Firm but measured. He knew his strength and used it in every way he should, and in none of the ways he shouldn't. When he lifted up Jen and lowered her onto the bed in the dim lit bedroom, her heart sped up and her nerved fine-tuned to every touch.

Sam climbed on top of her, his shirt already off, and she gripped his solid biceps like handlebars on a dirtbike. Her world existed inside that small space between them. They kissed and all the worries and uncertainties in the world above them were gone. Would their relationship last? Would Sam run off after he graduated? Would he not graduate and go nowhere? Where would she go? Was she really going to join the fucking Marines? None of that mattered then. It was just Sam and Jen.

At some point, he put her on her hands and knees and got behind her. She looked up as he went inside and she saw the dead body watching over both of them.

Jen didn't scream, but scrambled off the bed like she'd touched fire. A series of profanities spilled from her mouth as she scurried to the floor opposite the body.

"What? What the fuck? What did I do?" Sam said.

From her spot of the carpet, Jen stabbed a pointed finger across the mattress. "Look! You fucking jackass!"

Why they didn't smell him when they first came down into the bunker, Jen never knew. But what changed the man from a man into a dead body was obvious. A Smith and Wesson .45 revolver defty hung from the half-gripped fingers of his right hand. The black and dried blood that coated his neck, chin and lower lip hinted at the entrance wound inside his open mouth. The volcano-like splatter-art on the ceiling, punctuated by a bullet hole in the paneling, made the path of the bullet clear.

The man's body was dressed only in socks and a pair of soiled boxers nearly hidden by his bulging belly and thick fat legs. His ankles were swollen and bluish, like the thin white socks were the only thing keeping the blood from pooling and his feet from bursting like water balloons. His eyes were open and protruding outward beyond the lids. Maybe it was the pressure of the bullet that pushed his eyeballs out and his pupils forward, or maybe it was an undead desire to watch the entertainment before him. To Jen, it seemed the later.

"No fucking way," Sam said.

"I'm out of this place. I can't believe I let you…" she said as she gathered her clothes and left the bedroom.

#

Jen sat on the couch in the living room next to her shotgun, fully dressed, rocking, waiting for Sam to come out of the bedroom. Eventually he came out shirtless, holding a few sheets of paper.

"He wrote a suicide note," Sam said. "Says we should put his body in the composter. Says no one will miss him."

"I'm not going back in that room," Jen said.

"He says no one knew this place existed but him. He thought he'd never be found down here."

"I don't care, Sam. I want to go home. Now."

Sam lowered the papers to his side. "There's a hatch that feeds into the composter right from the kitchen. I saw it earlier. The least we can do is follow his wishes."

"I'm not touching that body."

"Fine," Sam said and walked up to Jen and the coffee table. He dropped the plain white paper, crosshatched by folds, onto the table. "I'll do it. Least you can do is read what he had to say."

Jen picked up the papers, but wouldn't look up. Sam went back into the back bedroom. She read:

To all the world,

You've been miserable. There is nothing outside worth living for.

Even worse, there is nothing inside I can tolerate, and the only

thing inside of this bunker, is me.

No one knows this place is here. The only life I've seen in the
months I've lived here is wildlife. The defense system keeps me
safe. The solar and geothermal power sources are working as they
should. The well and drain field provide me with water and
plumbing. The compost bin will fertilize the ground for a garden. I
have enough canned goods and shelf-stable food to last me. All I'm
lacking is the will to live that long.

Sometimes I wish someone else was down here with me.

If you find me, put my body in the composter and let it bury me.
Then consider using one of the guns on yourself. Don't hesitate and
pull the goddamn trigger. There is nothing outside of this bunker
living for, and there is nothing inside.

Good bye,

Dean

Jen looked up to see those swollen vein-laced ankles being dragged into the
kitchen. Sam grunted as he pulled and heaved the mass. Weight flopped on the kitchen
floor. Doors opened. Hatch clasps unlatched. More moans and movement of wet
matter. Jen noticed a trail of slime glistening off the hallway and kitchen floor like a
giant snail had migrated from one spot to another.

She heard Sam close up whatever access panel in the kitchen led to the
composter. Then he washed his hands, took his time and dried them. He came into the
living room.

"There's really not much of a mess in the bedroom. I think this place has a
constant working air exchanger. I'm guessing that's why he didn't smell. He's gone
now though," Sam said.

"He doesn't feel gone," Jen said.

Sam sat down on the couch next to Jen and put a hand on her thigh. "You
know, it's too bad for him that he shot himself. I mean, it's his loss. This bunker… We
really could stay here now if we wanted."

She looked at him.

"Think about it. He said it himself, no one knew he was here. He had supplies for years. There's food, water, electricity, entertainment. Why would we leave here? To go back to what we had? Worrying about what to do after high school? Finding jobs, paying rent, college... I mean Jesus, Jen. You were talking about joining the fucking Marines!"

"You can't be serious."

"Look. I get it. That was like, super gross. But it's gone now and we're better off than before we found him. Now we know this place is ours and no one else's. He's in the composter. I'll paint the walls, patch the hole. It will be like he was never here."

"He was watching us have sex."

"Think of him as a grandpa who left us this as an inheritance."

"I think I'm going to be sick," Jen said and got up.

Not that she wanted to go anywhere near the bedroom ever again, but the bathroom had to be off of the same hallway. She ignored the snail-slime trail and opened the door opposite of the bedroom door.

The room was dark. She felt for a light switch, flicked it on, and nothing happened.

"Did you hear that?" Sam asked from the living room.

Jen flicked off the dysfunctional light switch. "What?" she said.

Sam waited a second. "Huh. It's gone now."

Jen felt for another lightswitch, found one, and flicked that on. One lone light bulb dangling from the ceiling came on. The room was small, about the size of a bathroom, but decorated with dozens of guns hanging from hooks and peg board. Assault rifles, handguns, shotguns, hunting rifles... even a blow gun. There were also knives, a bundle of rope, a few tasers, nunchucks, and a full length gleaming ninja sword.

There was a workbench on either side of the room. The bench on the right was stocked with ammo. Loaded magazines. Boxes of cartridges. Loose rounds laying on the wood surface. The left bench housed a control panel with various buttons, knobs, switches and controls. There were six monitors embedded into the wall, each screen was popping to life and showing a part of the bunker's interior. After a few seconds, the image would switch to a view outside of the bunker, then back to the interior. The kitchen, the entryway, the living room, the bedroom.

"Oh jesus. We were on camera," Jen said.

"Whoa," Sam said, behind her now. "That's a lot of guns. Is that a katana? What's this light switch do?"

"I don't know. Sam, let's get out of here."

"I hear that noise again," he said.

"This place is creeping me the fuck out. You can stay with the dead guy if you want but I'm out," she said and pushed past him.

"Jen, come on. Look at this place," Sam said. "You seriously can't just walk away from here and pretend this place doesn't exist."

"Sam, there was a dead guy in the bedroom!"

"Yeah, well, that's his bad luck. But this bunker… This place has everything we could ever want. It's the solution to all our problems! How many times have we laid in bed together and wished we didn't have to get up to go to school or to work or to whatever other bullshit the world had waiting for us?" Sam said.

"Sam."

"You said it yourself. We can live here. Just you and me. In peace and quiet. Like a legit man and wife."

"I'm sorry, Sam. I'm leaving," Jen said. She marched from the gun room back over the snail-slime trail and back into the living room.

"Jen?"

She didn't stop, but picked up her shotgun off the couch as she headed for the stairwell leading back to the surface.

"Jen!" Sam called.

She was already heading up the stairs. She shoved open the cellar door and squinted back the blinding sunlight. She continued up and took a few steps into the clearing before her eyes adjusted to the light and what she saw stopped her in her tracks.

A pack of five timberwolves had gathered there. They were an untamed mix of white and brown fur, long legs of sinew and bone, yellowed teeth and golden reflective eyes. The biggest of them, the alpha male with a large hunchback, was nearing the deer carcass. The others turned their snouts towards Jen and the closest one loosed and long deep growl.

The heavy caliber machine gun fire that ripped over Jen's head and into the clearing silenced the growling wolf. Tracer and armor piercing bullets zipped inches over her head and punched into the tall grass and dirt, sending black plumes skyward. Jen screamed and crumpled to the ground, not hit by any bullet but terrorized off her feet. Her shotgun fell into the grass and was forgotten. She turned to scramble on all fours back to the cellar doors. She looked up and saw a .30 caliber Browning machine gun had emerged from behind a trap door embedded in the bunker's mound. The machine gun panned left and right, devoid of a human gunmen, scanning for motion.

The wolves had scattered, abandoning the dead growler.

Jen took no chances and crawled back to the cellar doors as fast as she could move. She nearly tumbled ass over tea kettle as she went down the stairs and back inside the bunker. Sam was waiting for her on the far side of the living room.

"I figured out what that switch is for," he said.

"You motherfucker, you could have blown my head off!" Jen yelled, her ears still ringing like she'd spent the day at a rock concert.

"How was I supposed to know it was attached to a motion sensored machine gun? Besides, did you see those wolves?" he laughed. "They would have ripped you limb from limb!"

"Turn it off. Right now," Jen said and looked back up the stairs.

"Jen, you're not leaving here."

Sam said the words, but it might as well have been the ghost of the dead man she saw sitting on the steps leading up to the cellar door. The man's ghost said just like he had in the bedroom. He wore only his socks and underwear, his belly and eyes distended and bulbous. His pupils were fixed on her. The snail-slime seeped from every orifice and skin fold.

She pushed herself the rest of the way down the steps and into the kitchen, against the fridge.

Sam went back into the gun room and flipped another switch. A thick steel door slammed down at the entrance to the stairs, sealing out the ghost, the wolves, and the rest of the world. She sat with her back against the fridge and panted. Sam came back from the gun room, opened the fridge and cracked a Keystone Light. The foam bubbled up out of the can's mouth and he slurped it up.

"There. Now nothing can come inside and nothing can go outside. Welcome to our new home, babe," Sam said.

#

Sam had chugged down the first beer fast and tossed the can onto the kitchen floor. Now he sat on an old rocking chair with the second beer in his hand and his shotgun across his lap. Jen sat on the couch, her face buried in her face, her mind spinning to sort the world straight again. She lifted her hands and peaked sideways.

The fat bloated corpse sat on the other end of the couch. His head was turned now so those popping eyes were fixed on Jen. The .45 revolver was still dangling in his hand, although Jen was sure if she reached for it her hand would move through thin air instead of touching the cold polished steel. She was afraid to try.

Sam didn't seem to notice the ghost. He kept on drinking another Keystone Light.

"Don't make it like this, okay?" Sam said. He drank. "You know I got nothing else. There's no jobs where anyone would hire me. I'm not going to get into college and even if I did, I couldn't pass the classes anyway. I can't standing living at home. My mom and dad are always so drunk and angry." He drank. "I can't join the army. I'm not brave like you, and I got flat feet." He drank. "Besides, down here things can be perfect. Now come on. Have a beer with me. We'll play some Paperboy."

There was something about his plea that tempted her. Why couldn't they have a nice afternoon of Keystone Light and Nintendo games? Then she glanced back over at the ghost. He had turned and fixed his eyes on Sam. He thick loose lips moved like he was mumbling whispers to Sam.

"You can't keep me here against my will," Jen said.

"Oh yeah? And what about that door? Or the machine gun? Or the wolves?" He drank. "I mean, I don't want it to be like that, but if I wanted to, I could keep you down here forever."

"And what about--" Jen looked down the couch, just one small cushion away, to the thick veiny corpse. He blinked. "What about the body we found?"

Sam laughed. The ghost made more silent mumbles in Sam's direction as if he were feeding Sam his lines. But it was Sam who spoke, "What about it? There's nothing we have to report to the police. He did it to himself and if anybody found him he wanted to be put in the composter. We did exactly what he asked."

Jen looked down at the suicide note.

"And what about the other things he wrote? 'Nothing outside. Nothing inside.' He said that."

More chuckles. Another long drag from the beer. More whispered words from the ghost that Jen couldn't hear. Sam crumpled the empty and tossed it to the carpet. "You really going to take advise from some fat fuck who suck-started a Smith and Wesson? Get real."

Sam got up, keeping his shotgun with him, and went to the fridge for a third beer.

Jen got up and moved in the opposite direction, towards the gun room. The body turned his head and watched her as she went past him. She ignored him.

The gun room control panel only had a few buttons, knobs and levers. She figured she could find the controls to the steel door and the remote machine gun in a matter of seconds. As soon as she was in the room she turned to the light switch that seemed broken before. Now she saw a label-maker tape that read "EXT DEF SYS." Exterior Defense System. She switched it off. Then she went in front of the monitors and the control panel and made a quick examination. Amongst the other buttons and knobs was a single-throw switch labeled "SECURITY DOOR." Before flipping that, she glanced up at the monitors.

In grainy black and white resolution, she saw Sam standing in the doorway to the gun room, shotgun raised up with one hand, fresh beer in the other. She was in the shot too, standing there at the control panel, paralyzed and afraid.

She looked over to the doorway, and there in real life was her boyfriend and the barrel of the 12 gauge. That hole at the end of the gun looked huge, large enough to consume her entire existence. Behind it were Sam's weeping red eyes, his non-aiming eye would open and close as he debated how he wanted to see her: full view, or beyond the bead of the gun.

Behind Sam was the ghost, slowly waddling closer, his lifeless jowls jostling as he came to a stop.

"Don't," Sam said. "Don't ruin this. I told you. This is all I got."

The fat ghost grinned and yellowish bile drooled out of his mouth, down his chin and drip drip dripped onto his naked belly.

"Besides, I'm not leaving, and you know you can't live without me," Sam said, smiling half-laughing like it was all in fun. "Your life outside of this bunker is just as dead-end and hopeless as mine. Without me, you have nothing, are nothing, will be nothing. We're only complete when we're together. We're meant to be together. Forever. Here, in this place."

Her hand was on the switch that would open the steel security door. All it would take was just the flick of the switch. She hesitated. A part of her knew what Sam was saying to be true. Her home life was as messed up as his had been. Together, they'd been the only stable thing in each other's lives. Separated?

"Sam, it wasn't supposed to be like this. You can't keep me here," she said and hit the switch. The grind of the raising steel security door rumbled through the bunker.

Sam's head turned towards the entrance. When he looked back to Jen, his eyes were fire-red. Sam bore his teeth. The ghost's smile grew wider. Did the ghost push Sam into her? If those pale bratwurst arms would have tried would they have passed through Sam like in the movies? Would they have thrust him forward? Maybe it didn't matter. Sam seemed motivate enough as he lunged into the gun room and shoved into Jen with the broadside of the shotgun.

She slammed into the back of the room. The peg board holding all of the weapons rattled and several items fell and tumbled to the ground. Jen fell too, down to the hard concrete floor. When she looked up, she saw stars and that wide bore of the 12 gauge.

"I could have given you everything down here! We could have had everything!" Sam yelled. He pumped the shotgun, ejecting a shell and chambering another. He flicked off the safety and closed his non-aiming eye. "If we can't live here together alive, you'll live with me dead."

Jen instinctively put a hand up, as if the thin flesh of her hand could stop the bird shot. Her other hand went to brace herself on the dusty concrete floor. It landed on the handle of the unsheathed ninja sword. She ducked down to put two hands on it. Sam fired the shotgun. Pellets plunged into her shoulder and one sliced through her ear. Jen didn't take the time to make sure she was still alive. Instead, she swung the ninja sword up like a bladed haymaker.

The glistening blade entered Sam just above the hip. It didn't stop until it after going through two rib bones. It didn't seem to stop him. He groaned, but pumped the shotgun and loaded another shell. The ghost behind a deep barking laugh. Jen pulled out the sword and plunged it through his stomach half-way to the hilt. Droplets of blood spat out from the wound on to Jen's arms and face.

This strike seemed to register in Sam's brain. He dropped the shotgun and looked down at the sword as she let go of it.

He looked up and met her eyes. "Why?" he asked, then tumbled over backwards, through the ethereal ghost. The fat dead man stopped laughing.

Jen picked herself up. She reached through the cold translucent dead man and turned off the "EXT DEF SYS" switch. Then she walked through him and over her boyfriend's body. The sword had been pushed back out of his torso when he landed and was resting there on the hallway carpet. She picked it up and left through the open bunker door.

Jen emerged from the bunker with blood oozing from her ear and shoulder. She couldn't hear a thing but didn't care. She could see the sunlight again and felt the fall breeze on her skin. Her shotgun was there waiting for her in the tall grass. She picked that up and held it in her right hand. The sword was in her left hand.

The wolves waited for her in the clearing. The alpha male locked her in its golden eyed gaze. Another wolf, another brave but foolish subordinate, growled. This time the growling didn't phase here. This time the machine gun wasn't scanning for motion over her head. This time nothing would stop her.

#

Inside the bunker, Sam bled profusely, but climbed up first to his elbows, and then to all fours. The fat fluidos ghost coaxed him with wordless chortles and grunts. Sam reached up for the "EXT DEF SYS" switch, blood smearing against the wall with each outstretched attempt. He knew his life was quickly fading away. If he wanted Jen down there in the bunker with him forever, he had to reach the switch.

He went back to all fours, tried to breath, tried to gain some strength. One more chance. He raised his arm and strained, his fingers wiggling out for the switch. It was just inches away. An inch. A half inch…

The Flea Circus

My voice has to show no signs of uncertainty.

I'm inside my trailer, rehearsing my lines inside my head. Even in here, just minutes before curtain call, I can still hear the rest of my troupe, whining and complaining. "Oh god damn it, will you people shut up!"

Ladies and gentlemen! Prepare yourself for a show yet unseen! For images your eyes will not understand! Prepare to be amazed at the spectacle set before you tonight for your viewing pleasure! For beasts and beauties! Grace and gallantry! For the joy of a child's laughter and the sorrow of broken souls! Ladies and gentlemen, children and children-at-heart! Welcome to the circus!

I have to focus. I have to summon all my confidence and bravery as I prepare myself for the big show. A touch of rouge on each cheek. A wisp of black under the eyes. Beeswax sculpts my moustache with just the slightest suggestion of a twist. I dust my lapels and shoot my cuffs. After all, this is show business and all the details must be attended to.

When the time comes for the opening spotlight to fall on me in the center ring, I can't be me. I can't afford to be this small and scared man, bankrupt and bullied by my own troupe, unsure if the audience could see past all the glamor and make-up. No. I have to be larger than life. I have to be the boisterous Ringleader, welcoming them to a world they could never imagine. It's what the people demand.

My thumb and finger wind a key and set my old flea circus in motion just as if it's a pocket watch. I imagine my human circus much like this old parlor trick. So simple but satisfying. Every invisible flea moving just as it should.

I close my eyes and rehearse my lines. As the words play in my ears, I can finally shut out theirs.

From parts unknown, bringing forth wild beasts from the Dark Continent, armed with nothing but his steeled nerves and a bullwhip! In the center ring, I give you the Lion Tamer!

Yes. Yes. That sounds good. My voice has to boom and fill every corner of the big top. It has to pump life into every vessel both in the stands and in the rings. The Lion Tamer will be up first. The kiddies alway love the lion. The king of the jungle! They'll jump at the crack of the man's whip and the lion's gnashing yellowed teeth. They'll awe at the illusion of instant reflexes and the Lion Tamer's dance with death.

I hear my troupe again, still moaning outside. "Shut your rotten mouths or I'll bury you, I swear it!" They should be in their places. The show is about to begin. Don't these people have any concept of showmanship? Of professionalism?

No. I'll only hear problems from the likes of them. The food is spoiled. The equipment is old. The animals are too vicious. The schedule is too demanding. The pay is too meager. Will they never cease? They have no idea how to run a show like this. They have no knowledge of the logistics involved. These hacks! These prima donnas! But I fixed them.

I put my hands over my ears to block out their nagging and concentrate on my next lines. After the Lion Tamer comes the Contortionist.

Lads and ladies! If you would be so kind as to direct your gaze to the far ring and the splendor of Madame Abagail, from the city of lights and romance: Paris, France! The Contortionist!

She is the most beautiful of them all. And so much more limber than before. I myself removed her human limitations. I worked her joints and muscles and sinew into the human sculpture she has become. So fluid now. She moves without any strain or sweat. A perfectly poseable doll. Her face ever gorgeous. But will they see the strings?

No. I have to eradicate doubt. I must remind myself that the audience is a willing participant. With their minds and with their eyes they perform just as much as my troupe. When they see the Lion Tamer react, they see his muscles and nerves fire on impulses from his brain. When they see the Contortionist twist, they see the long hours of her training. When they see the Sisters on the trapeze, they see their skill. I have to have at least as much faith as they.

I have to focus on my lines and ignore the voices.

I humbly present to you now, from the mysterious land of rupees and riches, tsars and revolutions, barren steppes and boundless wilderness... Behold! The Sisters Emerencia high above your seats on the trapeze, performing without a net!

The trapeze! A fan favorite! And so easy to work the strings. My god, they almost pull themselves. Yes. Yes. This will work. This will do more than just work. This will be the best performance the world has ever seen! And it is all because of me!

How can I doubt myself? Haven't I already proven myself stronger and more willing than all the rest? Haven't I done all the work to bring this to be? It was me! Just last night I visited each one of them while they slept. I am the one who made them better than they ever could have been in life. I was the one who pushed them beyond their natural limits. I was the one who shucked them of their mortal burden and silenced their all too human flaws.

My suit and makeup are all in place. Every stitch, stroke and detail are just so. Like the clowns and the mimes and the strong man and the stilt walkers, everything is ready now. All the ropes are taunt.

I brush past my old flea circus on the way out of my trailer. I have to thank it for the inspiration. Those tiny invisible fleas helped me see the future of this all too human show. But I have to leave childish things to children. I grab my stove pipe hat. My shined Jack boots echo down the steps of my trailer.

"Everything okay, boss? Who were you yelling at in there?" McFarlane, the chief stagehand, says to me. We picked him up outside of an asylum I believe. Such a willing partner.

"Nevermind that. They can't hear me anymore anyway," I tell him. As we march across the grounds, we duck under and step over the network of ropes and anchors. "Have all the preparations been made? Are all the gears wound?"

"Everything's set," McFarlane says.

When I speak to him again, my voice isn't my own. It is strong and loud and commanding. The voice of the Ringleader. "Excellent! It is imperative that none of you miss a cue! Every string must be pulled at precisely the right moment!"

"You got it, boss," he says, and I trust him.

I enter the big top. All the lights are down. I make my memorized way to the center ring through the darkness. The crowd is full of chatter and murmurs, excitement and anticipation. Only their energy can truly silence the whining and crying and screaming of my troupe now. I will play them like a puppet master. The crowd. The troupe. All of them. I'll pull all their strings!

"Ladies and gentlemen! Children and children-at-heart! Prepare to be amazed by the spectacle set before you! Tonight, you are willing participants as only your eyes and imagination can truly bring this show to life! Feats to amaze! Visions sure to dazzle! Mysteries guaranteed to confound the mind! Behold the wonders from around the globe! Welcome to the Cooper and King's Cavalcade Circus!"

Do they notice the wires? The seepage from the Contortionist's limbs? The breathless still lungs of the trapeze artist? The blood stains on the acrobat's costume? Do they notice McFarlane and his crew yanking and working the ropes in rhythm with the movements of the clowns? Can they see through the grease paint on my face to the cowardly man underneath?

I look into their beautiful sparkling eyes, and I see they believe!

The Hum

Barkley smelled the demon before I did. His hound-dog nose could detect the sweet smell of fried bacon five miles away. For him, smelling the demon just a city block down had to be like huffing in ammonia.

He howled, not loud but low and deep, his Basset-snout pursed to the night air.

For that moment, his howl overpowered the hum. But as soon as he finished, the hum returned. It was a constant rumbling white noise. Always there in the background, distracting and paining me. I wished to God every day that it would go away and I could have that simple clarity so many other people enjoy. I think Barkley could hear the hum too, but that wasn't what was bothering him right now.

The demon was one block down, across 6th Street. He looked like a man, mostly, wearing blue workman's coveralls with a white oval name patch that I've never been close enough to read. He had coke-bottle glasses and long greasy hair the hung well past his shoulders. He lurked in the shadows, usually keeping some distance away from me, especially when the hum was the loudest. When he drew near, the hum grew quiet. Everything grew quiet, especially before he killed.

"Easy, boy," I told Barkley.

He looked up to me with his big droopy eyes. Barkley was my three year old basset hound and my service dog. He had the little blue vest of a service dog, the face of an old dog, and the energy of a pup. He gave me a quiet "Chuff," and walked forward till his leash was taunt. Then he let out an impossibly bassy growl.

"I see him," I said.

The demon was waiting at the crosswalk for the light to change, hands in his pockets, head down, those penetrating eyes peering over his thick glasses. His lower jaw was slack. The hum quieted. What was he up to tonight?

The light changed. The demon shuffled across Main Street away from me.

I looked up at the lights at our intersection. It was "Don't Walk" across 6th Street, but "Walk" across Main. I decided to cross Main and catch up with the demon over on Madison. We had to keep him in our sights, had to be ready if he decided to strike.

"Come on, boy," I said and tugged on Barkley's leash.

He led me across the crosswalk, galloping and flopping his ears like Dumbo. When we hit the opposite curb we kept up our pace. I lost sight of the demon when we left Main Street, but we would pick him up again as soon as we hit Madison. I was sure Barkley still had his scent. He ran with purpose.

The two-story brownstones blocked our view of the demon, so we kept on. Past the tattoo parlor. Past the VFW. Past the antique shop. When we got to Madison and looked up towards 6th Street, there was no sign of the man in blue coveralls. He must has stopped somewhere between blocks. The hum was still subdued, but it was getting louder, which meant he was getting away.

"This way," I told Barkley and tugged on his leash. He resisted at first, but gave in. We headed up Madison towards 6th.

We passed a few drunks coming out of Ernie's Pub. Barkley barked at them, warning them about the demon, but they ignored us and went on talking about women and sports and politics. This was old downtown, populated by bars and gun shops and the like. No one here was tuned into the hum or the demon. Not like me and Barkley. They wandered through the night ignorant and blind.

We got to the corner of 6th and Madison. No demon. No drunks. A few cars passed by. Barkley's snout found more compelling things to smell on the light post and in the garbage can chained to it. The hum was back to full volume.

"Shit," I said.

There was a pawn shop half a block up named "Pawn Shop." Its neon light flickered on and off, emitting a "zit zit zit" sound. Maybe the demon had slipped in there. I doubted it, but it was worth a shot.

As me and Barks pushed through the door, a bell chimed. I looked up at the big bulbous mirror hanging in the corner and saw only me and Barkley as he sniffed an audio mixing board on the bottom shelf. No sign of the demon. No sign of anyone else.

"Hello?" I called.

Barkley chuffed. The hum was louder in here.

"Yeah. We're open," I heard a voice call back. A female voice. Pretty, but not all that kind.

Every square inch of wall and display shelf was buried in random human detritus. Rock instruments. Audio components. Old sporting equipment. DVDs. Tiny Limoges statues. Board games marked with handwriting on masking tape that read "Missing Pieces!" We moved towards the back of the shop in the direction of the woman's voice.

And like someone flicking off the light switch, the hum was gone.

I've never not heard the hum. In the city. Out in the country. At home. In cars... I hear it even in my sleep. Now, as if the hum's master had snapped his fingers for silence, it was gone. I could hear everything crystal clear. No distortion. No distraction. I imagine for a non-hearer of the hum, it would be the difference between sounds underwater and above water.

And just like that, it came back. Instantly. No fade in or out. Like the flick of a switch.

And then gone again.

The effect stopped me in my tracks, halfway towards the back of the pawn shop. It dawned on me that something in the shop might be the cause. I picked my feet up and kept moving as the hum was repeatedly clicked on and off.

I came around a rack of old romance novels and saw the girl behind the counter. About my age. Sloppy ponytail. Glasses. She had a device in her hands she glared down at. The device had a switch and when she flicked it, the hum died. She flicked it again and the hum was on again. Then she flipped it back and forth like a man testing a light switch that doesn't work.

"Excuse me," I said. The flicking of the hum on and off and on and off was driving me nuts. "Excuse me. What is that?"

"Huh?" she said, looking up for the first time.

"That thing in your hand, what is that?" I said.

She held up the device like it was nothing. The face she made said, "This old thing? This thing that could remove the source of your eternal torment? Oh nothing. Nothing at all." That wasn't what she said though. What she said was, "A guitar tuner?" Asking me as if I'd never heard of a guitar tuner before.

"Can I see it?" Oh god, did I want to see it.

"Fine. It's broken though. It only registers a low F note. All the time. Whenever it's on," she said flipping the switch and the hum off and on again. "It's garbage."

"No!" I said, a little too eager. The hum was still on. If she'd just hand it over... Oh god, the joy of no hum! "I mean, no. I can fix it. I fix things."

"Is that a dog?" she asked.

Barkley barked affirmative.

"He's my service dog. That's how come he's got the vest," I said.

"Oh. But, you're not blind. Are you?" she said and went looking into my eyes like an optometrist.

"No, he's for my anxiety. I'm a hearer," I said.

"A what?"

"A hearer. I hear the world wide hum," I said. I hated explaining it, but I was practiced at it. "It's a global phenomenon. Millions of people across the world hear it. I'm one of them."

"A hum?" she asked.

"Yeah. Imagine a garbage truck idling a block away from you wherever you go. Most days I can ignore it. Other days I can hardly stand it. I stay in bed and listen to music as loud as I can just to try to drown it out. That never works though. Doctors say it's psychosomatic, whatever that's supposed to mean. But that's why I got Barkley here," I said and ruffled up his head, flapping his ears all around.

He howled.

"Is he supposed to bark like that?" she asked.

"He's still in training. He's my dog," I said. "I have a prescription for an actual service dog, but the waiting list to get one is a mile long. So I got Barkley. We don't need one of their fancy trained dogs anyway. Do we, boy?"

He must have gotten bored with us humans. He pulled at the leash to go smell something else. I let him go.

"Can... Can I see the..." I gestured to the device in her hand.

"Oh," she said. "Yeah. Sure. Like I said, it doesn't work but if you think you can fix it, go for it."

She handed me the device. I was tempted to hit the ON/OFF switch as soon as it was in my hands, but I'd lived with the hum my whole life. What was a few more seconds?

It was a guitar tuner with a LED screen. The screen showed a gauge and a needle that could point between -40 and +40. Below the gauge were the letters A through F. Right now, the F was circled and the needle wavered between -10 and 0. As the electronic needle danced, I heard the pitch of the hum rise and fall in sync with the needle.

I clicked it off. The LED screen went blank. The hum was gone.

"So?" the girl asked, her voice as clear and clean as water from a brook.

"So..."

"Can you fix it?" she asked.

"Oh. Yeah. Totally," I said.

"Sweet. I bought it for five bucks. You fix it and bring it back and I'll pay you ten," she said.

"I can have it?" I asked.

"It's no good to me broken. If you can't fix it, toss it. I was about to throw it away before you came in," she said.

"Thanks."

"Thank you," she said, pulling out her cell phone and going back to whatever it was she was doing before me and Barkley walked into her life.

"Rita," I said.

She looked down at her nametag. "Yeah. Boss makes me wear it," she said and set her cell phone back down. "So what's your dog's name?"

"Barkley," I said.

"Do you call him that because he barks so much?"

"What? No. Because he's Sir Charles. Charles Barkley. You know, like the basketball player," I said.

She laughed. "His ears touch the ground when he walks. How is he like a basketball player?"

At that, Barkley howled long and loud from over by the car stereos.

"Yeah, you tell her, Sir Charles," I said.

She laughed again. He was working his charm. She was foolish to resist. "Can I pet him? I mean, I know you're not supposed to pet working dogs but…"

"Yeah, you can pet him. But I gotta warn you, if you rub his belly he'll love you for the rest of your life," I said.

She came around the counter and patted her thighs and called for him. Man, with the hum gone it was so much easier to focus. So much easier to talk and laugh and be funny. As Barks came lolloping up the aisle towards this girl named Rita for his belly rub, I couldn't help but smile. He came to her, rolled over and wiggled his short stumpy legs at her. She gave him the best belly rub he'd had in days.

"Does he do any tricks or anything? Does he play fetch?" she asked.

"No. He's never been really interested in fetch or roll over or any of that other stuff."

"So what brings you guys out this late at night," Rita asked.

"We're…" I hesitated. How could I make this not sound crazy? "We're looking for somebody. Maybe he came in here."

I pulled out my phone and squatted down next to her and Barkley. I opened the photo app and flipped through some pics until I found the demon. He looked like a normal man in the picture, a local loser with some blue collar job that paid shit. I showed it to her.

"Have you seen him?" I asked.

She shook her head no.

"Well, if you do, get away. He's dangerous," I said.

"Well, we're open twenty four hours, so I'll keep my eye out," she said. "I get off around six in the morning. You know 6th Street Station? The bar just down the block?"

"Yeah I know it," I said. Barkley was bored again and went running off down another aisle.

"They have a third shift happy hour. Will they let your dog in there?"

"They have to. It'd be like telling a paralyzed person they couldn't bring in their wheelchair."

"Um. He's taking a dump on the carpet," she said.

I looked and sure enough, Sir Charles was arching his back and getting ready to plop a steamer right next to the vinyl record collection. "Barkley! No!"

He stopped. Thank god he stopped before anything came out.

"I better get him outside," I said.

"Good idea," Rita said. "So… See you in the morning?"

"At 6th Street Station," I said.

"Six in the morning," she said.

"Got it." I picked up Barkley's leash and led him toward the door. This dog was a chick magnet, sure. But he was also a turd dispensing ticking time bomb.

"And your little dog too," she said.

"For sure!" I said, pushing open the door.

"You never told me your name," she called.

"James!"

"See you James! Bye Barkley!"

We stepped out onto Sixth Street. The normal buzz of a city at night filled my ears. The bars were closing and the drunks were coming out like cockroaches. They laughed and shouted at each other. Traffic was picking up too. But still no hum. I walked Barkley down a ways away from the pawn shop for him to do his business. I had his doodoo bags in my pocket. Doodoo bags and that guitar tuner.

Barkley hunched over the concrete in the alcove of an empty store front. I pulled out the roll of doodoo bags and the guitar tuner from my pocket. No hum. It was heavenly. The only time things were ever this quiet was when the demon was about to kill.

The demon... I looked up. Sixth Street Station, the bar where I was supposed to meet Rita, was maybe fifty feet up the sidewalk. A small crowd of people were gathered there by the curb, waiting for a cab or a ride. They were half in the bag. Laughing. Oblivious. The man in the blue coveralls stalked up behind them.

"No," I muttered.

He was changing. His posture curled from an upright man to a creeping wolf. Horns grew out from that filthy black hair. The nails on his fingers extended out from each tip like slow greasy switchblades. The blue coveralls turned to tattered shreds. His body smoked. His fangs forced back his lips and drool glistened as it strung down to the sidewalk.

The traffic light over Sixth Street turned green. Cars went blasting by. The demon crept behind the small crowd.

Barkley pinched it off and almost pulled his leash from my hand as he moved towards the corner. I fumbled with the guitar tuner.

The demon picked one out of the herd and shoved. A woman was ejected out of the crowd and into the street, right in front of a rushing Ford F150. I saw her head explode. The Ford's brakes locked up. The dead woman's body bounced around under the truck. People screamed.

I flicked the switch on the guitar tuner. The hum snapped back on. The demon turned toward me and Barkley. He looked at me dead in the eyes and hissed like a snake. Then he turned and ran back down Main Street, out of sight.

Barkley was barking and howling like mad. People kept on screaming down by the "accident." Cries to God. Cries for someone to call 911. Cries of innocence from the driver of the truck. Audio pandemonium.

I stood there shaking, knowing it was my fault for turning off the hum. My heart was pounding. My nerves were short-circuiting through my body. My anxiety was going haywire. The hum was louder than ever.

I had to leave. I couldn't take it.

#

My apartment was over on Cleveland, three floors up in a mostly empty brownstone shithole. Until I got Barkley his service dog vest I had to sneak him in and out each day. Now I traded all the sneaking around for arguments with the landlord over Barkley's legitimacy and medical necessity. I couldn't live without Barkley. He was all I had.

I was all he had too.

I laid on my couch, head turned toward a TV I wasn't listening to. My blankets were under me and hung down on the floor where Barkley laid on them too. I had a beer in my hand. I'd probably fall asleep with it half full, if I could fall asleep at all.

The hum was louder than ever. Why wouldn't it be? The demon had gotten his. He'd lurk and wait before he struck again. Or until I turned the guitar tuner back on. It sat on my coffee table, turned off and letting the hum have its way with me. Barks whined on the floor next to me. It was affecting him too. I was sure of it.

"It's okay, boy. I hear it too," I said.

I was too late. One goddamn second too late. If I would have flicked off the guitar tuner one second earlier the hum would have chased the demon away and that woman would still be alive. I couldn't get the sight of her head colliding with the truck's bumper out of my mind. The image was as persistent as the hum and just as tormenting. I replayed the impact, and then the screams. Then came the hum and the demon's hiss. Then Barkley's howl and the ambulance's sirens. And of course Barkley and the ambulance had to turn it into a competition. He howled till his throat was dry and we were back to the apartment.

What a night.

And I was supposed to wake up in the morning to meet Rita.

Everything had been going so well. Why didn't I turn off that goddamn guitar tuner? Why'd I have to ruin it? Why did it have to be the hum or death? No one else had to make that kind of decision, and no one else would understand the temptation of turning the tuner back on. The sweet relief of no hum! I didn't believed for a minute that the doctors and scientists were ever going to find a cure. I had accepted life with the hum, but to live without it for just those few minutes with Rita… The stars had aligned. Things were finally going good for me. Why did I ever leave that pawn shop?

I laid there with the guitar tuner within reach on the coffee table. My beer slowly warmed. Barkley whined. Those big radar-dish ears. The hum had to be even louder for him. Poor boy. A lot of nights he'd lay awake and chew on the legs of the coffee table while I slept on the couch above him. Tonight, he was awake. I hung my arm down and rubbed his head to calm him. Petting him relaxed me too. Somehow, I managed to nod off, hum and all.

I woke up to Barkley barking at the apartment window. Something had upset him. He had his paws on the window sill and he was really going to town. My beer had fallen to the floor and he must have he licked it up. But it wasn't the beer. There were more ambulance sirens outside. I grabbed the guitar tuner, checked to make sure I hadn't turned it off in my sleep. I hadn't.

"Barkley, quiet," I said.

The pounded and swearing from upstairs would start soon. He wasn't even that loud. The hum was loud and growing louder still. Barkley kept barking. The sirens grew closer, the Doppler Effect raising their pitch.

"Barkley! Quiet!" I said.

He ignored me. With each bark he fogged the glass.

"Shut that fucking dog up!" the asshole upstairs yelled. "No dogs allowed in the apartment!"

"He's my service dog, you prick!" I yelled back. "My service dog!"

Barkley barked nervous woofs. He was scared. Anxious. These assholes weren't helping. The hum was so loud now, everything else was a whisper compared to it. The guitar tuner was still in my hand.

It was a tiny switch. Just a little grippy part flush with the side of the case. One little push and it would all go away. The hum would die and Barkley would be good and I could sleep so I could wake up to see Rita in the morning and everything would be cool. One little flick of a switch.

"Shut that mutt up, or I'll put a fucking bullet in his head!" the neighbor yelled.

"Don't you say that! Don't you fucking say that you fucking prick!" I was yelling now. Lines had been crossed. The hum throbbed in my ears. "Can't you motherfuckers hear that!? Can't you hear it? Every goddamn day every goddamn minute I can't fucking take it and you fucking assholes don't you ever come near my dog! Do you hear me? Don't you ever come near my dog you fucking assholes!"

"Shut the fuck up!" Others were getting involved now. The whole damn building was waking up. It didn't matter. Barkley wasn't going to stop. Not for them.

"We're trying to sleep!"

"Shut that dog up!"

"Fuck you!" I yelled. "Fuck all you! Come here, Barkley! Come here, boy!"

He pushed away from the window and dropped his ears down, ashamed he'd started so much ruckus.

"Come here," I said and he did.

I sat on the floor and he put his head in my lap. I leaned against the couch and soothed him. He whimpered and I told him it was okay, that I heard it too, that I'd never let them hurt him. It was awhile before I realized the guitar tuner was still in my hand. It scared me, seeing it there in my palm, tempting me to find true silence with the flick of a switch. Like Frodo slipping on the One Ring.

That poor woman.

I set the guitar tuner back on the coffee table, as far from me as I could reach. The hum rambled on.

"It's okay, boy. We're going to be okay," I told him, but didn't believe it.

#

We woke up like that in the morning, me slumped against the couch and Barkley in my lap. My cell phone alarm was going off but I barely heard it over the hum. Still, I fumbled with it and eventually turned off the alarm.

Fifteen forty five. Shit. Sixth Street Station was a good ten minute walk from the apartment, which left me five minutes to make myself look and smell like I hadn't slept on the floor with my dog. The sun was coming through the apartment window like a laser beam aimed for my brain. That was alright though. It would help me wake up.

"Barkley. Time to wake up, boy. We gotta get moving."

By the time we got up and dressed and over to Sixth Street Station I was six minutes late. It was a chill morning with a wind that cut through my clothes and a sunrise that cut through my corneas. The hum had only gotten more painful. A couple of times during the walk over I had to check for blood coming out of my ears. It felt like there was bleeding, but when I checked my finger it always came away clean.

When Barkley and I came to Sixth and Main he tugged at his leash to smell the wet spot in the road just in front of the bar.

"Come on, boy," I said and pulled him towards the door.

The place was mostly empty. I'd been in there before but it was weird seeing it in the daylight. Most nights, everything seemed wet and shining. Now, I could see the dust hanging in the sunlight above the pool tables and high top tables. The people seemed dusty too. The bartender was an angry-looking man. There were some tired men in work clothes at a table by the pool tables. The one waitress looked like she should be getting a discount breakfast down the street rather than serving beers.

"Hey, you can't bring a dog in here," she said.

"He's a service dog," Rita spoke up from one of the nearby high top tables. "You have to let him in. He's like a wheel chair."

Barkley woofed. The old waitress took one look at him in his little blue vest and said, "Huh."

Rita waved us over, and we came to the table. I looped Barkley's leash under the leg of my stool and plopped my butt on the seat. I looked up at Rita and she looked mostly the same as last night. Same clothes. Same ponytail and glasses. Her eyes a little more baggy after a full shift, but just as chipper and happy to see Barkley. Me on the other hand...

"Wow. You look like shit," she told me.

"Thanks," I said. Why does death and the hum have to haunt me wherever I go? I just wanted to be normal. I just wanted her to like me. "Me and sunlight don't always get along."

"Hey, I'm a nightwalker and a day drinker, so I know how that goes," Rita said.

The old waitress was making her way over to our table. "What will you have?"

"Beer, I guess. Whatever's cheapest," I said. My hand went instinctively into my pocket. It found the guitar tuner there. My thumb fell on the ON/OFF switch, but I didn't move it.

"Two fer one's on domestics," the waitress said. "Third shift happy hour till eight."

"Yes. That. Two for both of us," Rita said, ordering for me and her. As soon as the waitress left, she turned to me. "There were all kinds of police and ambulances outside the shop after you left. I was worried that maybe you got hurt."

"No. That wasn't me. Some lady. She just stepped out into traffic I guess," I said. And as fast as that, the beers came back. Four cans, each with their tops popped. "I don't think I've ever started drinking this early before."

"Yeah. Well, you can't drink all day if you don't start in the morning. Cheers!" she said and picked up one of the cans. She clinked her can against one of mine, only it sounded more like a "thunk" than a "clink." She drank. "So are you looking for that guy again today?"

I nodded. Barkley woofed. I saw the group of men over by the pool table glare at him. The hum felt like marbles being crammed into my ear canal.

"So what did this guy do?" Rita asked. "Does he like owe you money or something?"

Again, how do I make this not sound crazy? I couldn't concentrate with the hum in my ears, not enough to make up a good lie. So I told a half-truth. "I think... I think he has an effect on the hum."

"The world wide hum. That's some weird shit," Rita said.

I sensed her doubt. "Most people when I tell them about the hum, they don't believe me. Think I'm making it all up. Sometimes I feel like they're the ones lying, that everyone can hear it and the whole world is just playing a big joke on me." I drank some of my beer.

She drank some of hers. This wasn't going well. She could tell I was a freak. And Barkley being down so low by the floor, his charm was out of range.

"So you hear it now?" she asked.

I nodded and when I did, emotions whelmed up in me. Maybe it was from sleeping on the floor, or seeing what I saw last night, or just how loud the hum was getting, but I was struggling to hold myself together. My hand was sweating against the tuner in my pocket.

If I turned it on just for a moment, just to compose myself and ease the pain, there's no way the demon would come. Not if I kept it short enough. He quenched his thirst last night. No way he'd come back this morning already. That's what I told myself anyway.

"It's all the time," I admitted. "But when I'm around you…" I gave in, unconsciously or maybe just subconsciously. It only took a moment of weakness. The slightest push of my thumb. The hum died. The bar turned quiet. I heard the conversation of the men by the pool tables. I heard the bartender clean and clink glasses. There was country music playing out of the jukebox. I looked up into her expecting eye. "But when I'm around you, it's like it goes away."

"Oh really?" she cracked a smile. "You're almost as charming as your dog. Almost."

"Well he's tough competition."

"True, but he did try to shit in my store so don't feel too good about yourself," Rita laughed.

There we go. Now I was back in the groove.

Then he walked through the back door of the bar, the door leading out to the smoker's patio. An ugly man in soiled blue coveralls, hair so black and filthy it looked wet, face drawn and limp like a double-stroke victim.

"You okay, dude?" she asked.

I didn't respond. Barkley stood up on four paws and aimed his snout across the bar as the demon moved behind the men near the pool tables.

"Look, we can do this some other time," Rita said. "You're just starting your day and probably weren't planning on tying one on at the crack of dawn. Most other guys aren't into breakfast beers either."

"No! It's okay. Really," I said. The damn tuner. Why did the switch hide from me when I needed it the most? I pulled the tuner out of my pocket, still keeping it below the table, found the switch and hit it. The hum returned. I looked over her shoulder and the demon was gone like a whisper in the wind.

"You good?" Rita asked.

"I'm good," I said. Ignoring the hum now was as easy as ignoring a mugging while trying to hold a conversation.

"You sure?"

"Yeah. I'm fine. Sorry," I said. Come on, James. Deal with it. Accept it. Say something to her. Something cool. "So, tell me about you. You don't hear the hum. You work in a pawn shop overnights..."

"Yeah, I got a weird life, I know. To be honest, I like the peace and quiet of working overnights. After bar close everyone just goes to bed. And the people who do come in to the shop between bar close and the crack of dawn, well, they're interesting. Sort of like you and Barkley here."

I squinted and ground my teeth as she talked. Tried to smile as my audio-torturer turned the screws. And before I even realized I did it, my thumb pushed the switch on the guitar tuner. Silence.

"My dad used to work there. He was a guy who liked to fix things. He'd take in all kinds of junk and try to repair it and sell it again," she was saying. I wasn't listening, even though I heard the words perfectly clear.

The demon didn't bother to return in human form. He arose behind the backs of the men by the pool tables like he'd taken an elevator up from hell straight through the floor. He looked the part. Fangs. Horns. Beady black pupils. Foot long razor finger nails.

Barkley was still on his feet. He woofed and growled. His snout pointed like an arrow across the bar.

"James?" I heard someone say.

The demon selected one of the men and rested his ten hideous long fingernails on the man's shoulders. The man started to cough and clutch the center of his chest. Of course his buddies didn't notice. He'd die right in the middle of them and they wouldn't bat an eye until his corpse hit the floor. I blinked and I saw the image of the woman being run down in the street. I couldn't let it happen again.

"James?" she said again.

I turned the guitar tuner off and the demon turned to dust and fog right before my eyes. The hum returned and muted everything else. Rita was saying more words, but I couldn't tell what they were. All I heard was that constant diesel engine rattling around inside my brain.

"I have to step outside. I have to take care of something," I said, maybe yelled, to her. I got off my stool and unhooked Barkley's leash from my stool. "Come on, Barks."

"James?" she called after me.

Enough was enough. I had to get away from people. I had to get the demon alone. I had to isolate him. I walked towards the men at the pool table. I looked at the floor as I walked past them, half expecting to see some ectoplasmic pool where the demon had disappeared. There was just dirt and old gum and litter. For good measure, Barkley sniffed the spot as we walked by.

I think I heard the men asking their buddy if he was alright. He said something about heartburn and that "motherfucking chili dog." They had no idea.

There was a short hallway with doors to the men's and women's rooms on either side. At the end of the hall was a metal door with the word EXIT above it in red lights. I shoved it open and Barkley and I stepped out to the smoker's patio.

The place was surrounded on all four sides by the walls of other buildings. There was some metal patio furniture set out. A few cigarette butt cans. Clear unlit Christmas lights hung overhead. No one else was around. I unclipped Barkley's leash and used it to lash the door back into the bar shut. He trotted out amongst the patio furniture and butt cans, sniffing everything as he went.

The hum followed me out, but somehow it shrank quieter. My mind found peace out there if only for a short reprieve. I knew it wouldn't last. Me and Sir Charles, we had business to tend to. I held the guitar tuner in my hand as I walked towards the back of the patio. I turned it in my hand, end over end, keeping my thumb away from the switch. When I'd walked as far as I could I turned to face back to the bar.

"Okay, Barkley. You ready, boy?" I said.

He woofed.

I steeled myself, then killed the hum.

Smoke that smelled like burnt hair and rotten eggs seeped up through the concrete joints in the patio. The demon self-exhumed out of the pavement and soot in full form. His clothes were billowing tatters of blue material. His face full of fangs and crowned with horns. His tongue dangled out of his mouth, flexed and ready to lick and taste. His hands were cupped upwards like he was ready to tear out my crotch with those nails. On his chest, the little white oval name patch was still just a little oval white name patch. It read, "Gary." He took a step towards me.

I held up the tuner like a crucifix warding off a vampire. "Stop!"

The demon held his ground. Barkley was going mad barking. Drool and froth expelled with each chomping woof.

"Give it to me, boy," the demon spoke, his voice an uncanny verbalization of the hum.

"Fuck you, Gary," I said. I didn't know who Gary was or if this thing in front of me ever was Gary, but if he was going to wear a name patch I was going to fucking use it.

The demon hissed. "You want me to have that. I know what it does. We can both have what we want," he said.

The sound of his voice, it rumbled in my ears just the way the hum did. It was tuned into a specific part of my brain, the part that registers pain, anger, and confusion.

"I can make it go away," the demon said. "Me and the hum. You'll never hear or see us ever again."

"I know what you do," I said.

Barkley did too. He circled around the demon like a martial arts master weighing his opponent, all the while barking and howling and salivating.

"What business is that of yours?" the demon asked.

I didn't have an answer. Why was it any of my business? "If I give it to you, what will you do with it?" I asked him.

"Leave it on. Let it kill the hum. I'll make sure it leaves you in peace. Isn't that what you want? A normal life?" the demon said. He moved closer to me. Glided over the concrete. His arms elongated and fingernails grew. Everything stretched towards the guitar tuner.

I was still holding it out like it was a talisman. It wasn't. If I let him, the demon would pluck it right from my fingers.

"You want it?" I asked.

"Yesssssss. Give it to me, boy," the demon said.

"You want it?" I asked again, a little more cheerful this time.

"It belongs to me," the demon said.

"You want it, boy?" I asked Barkley.

He woofed, just once.

"Fetch!"

I tossed the tuner over the demon's head. Gary watched it as it arced through morning breeze. As it came down, Barkley leapt up and caught it in mid-air. He brought it down and shook his head with it in his teeth like it was a squirrel he'd finally caught. It took him two chomps to crack the tuner's case. Another chomp and the LED screen cracked and the circuit board snapped into pieces. The batteries fell to the ground. The hum returned.

The demon cried out, turning the sound of the hum stereophonic with his voice. It didn't last long though. Gary howled and bitched and moan and turned back into soot and dust. When the smoke cleared, Barkley was laying down and munching on the plastic shell of the guitar tuner.

"Good boy, Barks," I said. "Now give me that thing. That's no good to eat."

#

I figured by the time I came back into the bar, Rita would be long gone. And if he left, so be it. I had Barkley and we had the hum and we'd make do. It was in my ears again, not nearly as bad as it had been before, but still there. It was always going to be there.

Rita was still at our table. She smiled when she saw us coming. I smiled too. Barkley, well, he was always sort of smiling.

"You're back," she said.

"Yeah," I said and let Barkley's leash go. He put his front paws up on her legs and she rubbed his dead. I couldn't yell at him. He deserved a good ear scratching.

"Feeling better?" she asked.

"Yeah, but I have to tell you something," I said and got serious for a moment. She got serious too. I pulled what was left of the guitar tuner out of my pocket and set it on the table. Wires. Pieces of circuitry. Plastic busted apart and covered in teeth marked. "I wasn't able to fix your guitar tuner."

She laughed and if only for a moment, it drowned out the hum.

About the Author

Joe Prosit writes Sci-fi, Horror, and Psycho fiction. He lives with his wife and kids in the Brainerd Lakes Area in northern Minnesota. If you're an adept stalker, you can find him on one of the many lakes and rivers, or lost deep inside the Great North Woods. Or you can just find him on the internet at www.JoeProsit.com and follow him on Twitter @JoeProsit for new releases and upcoming events.

Made in the USA
Monee, IL
12 June 2023